The Front

Flyover Fiction

SERIES EDITOR: RON HANSEN

The Front

Journey Herbeck

UNIVERSITY OF NEBRASKA PRESS   LINCOLN

Library of Congress
Cataloging-in-Publication Data
Names: Herbeck, Journey, author.
Title: The front / Journey Herbeck.
Description: Lincoln: University of Nebraska
Press, [2021] | Series: Flyover fiction
Identifiers: LCCN 2020057470
ISBN 9781496225993 (paperback)
ISBN 9781496228406 (epub)
ISBN 9781496228413 (pdf)
Subjects: GSAFD: Suspense fiction.
Classification: LCC PS3608.E726
F76 2021 | DDC 813/.6—dc23
LC record available at
https://lccn.loc.gov/2020057470

Set in Stempel Garamond by Laura Buis.
Designed by N. Putens.

To my nieces and nephew, and to the world they will need, but not the world we have left them.

ACKNOWLEDGMENTS

I started writing this novel with my nieces and nephew in mind, thinking my way through the relationships we had developed during their visits here in Montana over the past few summers, especially on the trip we took up through Browning so they could see the Indian Relays and experience the Rocky Mountain Front. Because of these familial bonds, and how they continue to grow, my first acknowledgement needs to be directed to the undeniability of family. We can be at our best or at our worst when protecting the bonds that connect us. Writing about family is encouraging and disheartening in equal parts, but I don't think I could write about anything else.

I need to acknowledge Courtney Ochsner and the University of Nebraska Press for validating the feelings I have for the characters in this book and the journey they must take. I had begun to think their journey might not matter, and now I have regained my belief that it does. Melissa Fraterrigo also gave this novel an important vote of confidence, for which I am grateful. Stan Rubin and Judith Kitchen created the Rainier Writing Workshop (RWW), where I felt welcomed and where they expected me to work hard and to be kind. While at RWW, Mary Clearman Blew, David Cates, Kevin Clark, and Kent Meyers showed me how to take as much of the writing environment with me as I could after my turn there was over. Meghan McClure and Andrew Bennett continue to help me remember what we started at RWW and continue to be generous with their time by offering to push my work where it needs to go. Meghan Bullard is the friend all writers dream of: sharp and caring with a knowledge of how words should go together, precise and unrelenting with an invaluable habit of returning whatever I send her within a week, replete with all the honest comments I needed to see. Thank you, Meghan. I need to thank Alison Wright, who always makes me feel what I write is pretty good, or at least good enough to keep working at, and who is a friend who will tell me what's right and what's wrong, and who encourages me as I work my way through both.

And all the rest is family—undeniably. My childhood nuclear family is still the only family I have, and, well, that still makes me a very fortunate person. My mom, my dad, and my two brothers are all still doing their best to show the youngest how to get down safely from the precarious positions in which he finds himself.

The Front

0   The reservoir was low. We put our things on the table and stood with our feet in the sun but with the shade of the shelter coming down over our heads, except for my niece. Shelly climbed onto the picnic table to be entirely in the shade, and she looked out and studied where the coast of the Tiber Reservoir had gone, putting her hand up to her brow to shield her eyes from the sun, which was already blocked by the shelter.

—Where's the water? my little niece asked. She kept her hand above her eyebrows, slowly panning left and right. She was a kid who could pretend herself into other realities, other environments, and now it looked like she was pretending she was a captain without a sea to captain anything on. There's no water, she said.

Dad sat on the concrete bench and started untying his shoes. Mom looked over at him. She had her hands perched on her hips. She sat down next to him and started untying her shoes. My sister kicked off her flip-flops and told her daughter to put on her bathing suit.

—I don't see any water out there, Mom, Shelly said.

—Get your bathing suit on, my sister repeated.

My niece lowered her hand from her brow and started looking through the bags on the picnic table.

—Here it is, she said and pulled the one-piece yellow suit out of a brown paper sack. Her grandma helped her out of her shorts and began pulling her shirt up over her head.

—Raise your arms, my mom said to her, and the shirt slipped off. Shelly pulled her hair away from her face.

I stepped on the heels of my shoes to remove them and peeled my socks off. I rolled my jeans up to my calves. Mom pulled the straps over her granddaughter's shoulders and patted her on her butt.

—All set, she said to her. Grab your uncle's hand.

—Thanks, Grandma. My niece reached out to me, and I helped her step down from the table, to the bench, to the cracked concrete floor of the shelter.

—Where's the water? Shelly asked again.

—It's out there, her mom said.

—I can't see it.

—Neither can we. Let's go.

My niece let go of my hand and she and her mom started down the trail that led to where we hoped the water would be. My mom, my dad, and I grabbed the cooler, the umbrella, and the chairs, and we followed them down the trail. Within a few yards the trail was gone and we walked where there should have been water but where now there were only scattered footprints preserved within dry mud. The prints looked fossilized, dating back a year, maybe a thousand years.

Shelly stopped and stood among the hardened footprints and looked around at them. She put her feet into the preserved footprints of someone who had stepped there before her. There were prints that walked toward the water and those that walked away. Shelly looked up at her mom, and her mom down at her. Thirty yards out the crusted lake bed turned moist and the footprints disappeared. A stench wafted up from this hot, wet substrate. Shelly looked out to where the stench came from, to where there were no more footprints. Her nose wrinkled at the smell.

—We still going? Shelly asked. Her feet were much smaller than the prints they stood in. She wriggled them back and forth, nestling deeper down, her left foot one big stride in front of her right.

My sister looked back at the three of us. Dad shifted a lawn chair that hung from one of his shoulders. Mom nodded.

We stepped from the dry mud into the muck, fluttering our hands up and down in the air to keep balance, each foot sinking slightly, each foot popping up out of the muck's suction. Between these countermovements, we each took quick glances up to where the water should have been. My niece's straight dark hair swung from shoulder to shoulder as she high-kneed her way slowly over the reservoir floor.

—There should be water here already, right? Shelly asked.

Her mom nodded.

Shelly unbalanced to her right, and her mom pulled her back in; Shelly unbalanced to her left, and her mom gently bumped her straight again with her hip.

—Have you ever seen so little water? Mom asked Dad. Dad had stopped and turned to look back at the truck.

—We haven't seen any water yet.

—So no?

—No, I've never seen no water, Dad said, still looking at the truck. Mom turned and looked at the shelter and the truck too.

—Everything okay back there? My sister pulled a lock of hair out of Shelly's mouth. Don't chew your hair, she said to her.

Mom turned around.

—Truck looks fine, she said, searching for the water of the reservoir again. Dad kept looking at it. It's fine, she repeated. He turned and braced himself to Mom and let her lead him through the muck.

—Is this a puddle? Shelly asked.

I looked up from the muck. My sister and my niece were standing in ankle-deep water.

—Must be a puddle, I said.

The water they stood in was dusty white. It extended out to the silver ripples of a mirage, which extended out to the blurred line between horizon and sky.

—Is this it? Dad asked.

—No, can't be, Mom said.

We walked up beside my sister and Shelly, all of us now with our feet in the chalky water. No tiny waves lapped at our ankles. The water stayed flat and still around us. I looked behind us to gauge the distance we'd walked. The picnic shelter and our truck were at an indeterminable distance, one floating above or below the other as another mirage played out behind us, distorting their locations within the hot air. I tried to squint through the strands of silver that wavered back on the shore. A hill should have been visible above the truck and shelter too, but it was somewhere within the mirage, erased by the thick waves that bent from the reservoir floor up into the sky.

—It's warm, my niece said.

I turned back around and she moved her foot left and right through the pasty water. A cloud of white spread where she arched her foot back and forth. She coughed and wiped the back of her forearm across her mouth. We all looked at her. Her mom asked if she was okay. She didn't respond and kept her eyes on the murky water.

—You can get in if you want, Dad told her.

We looked at him.

—If you want, he said.

—How would I get in? Shelly asked.

—What do you mean? Dad said.

—There's no way in. It's too shallow. The water doesn't go anywhere.

—You're not getting in, my sister told her.

Mom shook her head, agreeing with my sister.

—I don't want to get in, Shelly said.

Mom unfolded a chair and sat down. The drive from Conrad to the reservoir was only about an hour, but it always seemed longer, none of the roads good. Mom let out a long breath. She placed the other chair on the reservoir floor beside her and brought her hand up to her forehead, like her granddaughter had done to shade her eyes back at the shelter. Brightness came at us from everywhere. The sun, the water, the pasty whiteness of the substrate that surrounded us. Wrinkles split from the corners of Mom's eyes, paralleling those across her forehead.

Shelly shook her hand free from her mom's and crouched down to look more closely at the water. She reached for a stick that was poking through the surface.

A bead of sweat fell from my forehead and ran down my eyelid and through my eye. It stung and I pulled up the end of my T-shirt to wipe it out. My vision blurred and I worked at my eye some more and then opened my eyes again and waited for the focus to come back. I blinked and waited some more. The faint murmur of the oil-rigs surfaced, rusty bolts squeaking against rusty washers. I couldn't see any of them, though, all of them hidden behind the mirages and within the blurs that covered my eyes.

—Don't touch the water, my sister said to Shelly.

—I'm not.

Dad wasn't looking at the water. He faced the parking lot and the truck again.

—Let's go, Dad said. He ran a finger across his forehead and flicked sweat onto the ground behind him. The truck was hidden behind the same silver ribbons that hid the oilrigs.

—Can you see it? I asked my dad.

He shook his head.

—We should go.

—Wait, Shelly said. She tugged at the stick some more. It was stuck in the mud below the water.

—Leave it, her mom said. We're going.

Mom leaned forward to stand up. Shelly pulled the stick out of the water.

—I got it. Shelly stood from her crouch and showed the stick to her mom. Pieces of lake gunk stuck to it.

—Give me that, her mom said and Shelly handed it to her. My sister went to toss it into the water and then stopped. She rolled it through her fingers. She shook some of the gunk off of it and wiped the rest off against her shorts. She held it for the rest of us to see.

—That's not a stick, Dad said.

My sister shook her head in agreement.

—What is it? Shelly asked.

—That's a bone, Mom said.

1

—Hey, I whispered, and nudged her shoulder.

Shelly didn't move. I rocked her gently back and forth. She only had a thin sheet over her, the other covers pushed to the bottom of the bed. The night had been warm. I nudged her shoulder again.

—Hey, she said. She rolled over onto her back and opened her eyes.

—We gotta go, I said.

—Where's Mom?

—She got picked up an hour ago. She's already at work.

—What time is it?

—Sun's almost up, I said. Six o'clock.

Shelly was sweating, her forehead reflected light from the hallway.

—You're hot, I said.

She nodded her head against her pillow.

—Can you get dressed while I get the truck ready?

—I'm thirsty, she said.

—There's a little water in the kitchen.

She swallowed hard, trying to clear her throat of phlegm. I pulled the curtain back from her window and dim light from the flares across the street fell over her through the bars and the ripped screen.

—How'd you sleep?

She closed her eyes and shook her head. Not very good.

—Sorry, I said.

She tried to make a smile that said *That's okay*, but it fell away before it could completely form.

—Can you get dressed?

She nodded her head against her pillow again.

—Right now? I said softly.

—Yeah. Her voice was quiet and sore.

—Okay. I stood up.

—We're going back to the reservoir, I said.

—We're having another adventure day? she said. Only half her words came out as sounds; the rest were only breaths.

—Yeah, another adventure day.

—Okay, she said, and she sounded interested in having an adventure. Shelly pushed herself up to her elbows.

—See you in five minutes?

—Can we go get some water?

—Get some in the kitchen, I said. Then we'll make more at the reservoir.

Her elbows slid out from underneath her, and she lay back in bed, disappointed. The reservoir water tasted bad.

—Hey, five minutes, I said. Her eyes were closed. She nodded her head once.

I walked down the hallway and saw Dad at the kitchen sink, leaning on it, his fingers on the edge of it, gripping it.

—Where you headed? he said.

—Hey, I said. You're up.

—I couldn't sleep, too hot. Where you headed?

—Back to the reservoir.

—What you looking for out there?

—We didn't get any water yesterday.

—You going to dig up those bones? he asked. I shrugged my shoulders. You shouldn't go out there, he said.

—We might get lucky.

My dad pulled his fingers flat against the inside edge of the sink in one long, anxious pull after another.

—What's up? I asked.

—Your sister called, he said. I hadn't heard any phones. She said there's a new point of revision east of the highway.

—Where?

—Lindero.

—We'll head north before that then, I said. He nodded.

—She said they were checking everyone.

—She get through all right? I asked.

—Yeah, fine. Because of her coworker. But they haven't done anything like that since the last change.

—Did she mention any others?

He stopped passing his fingers over the white porcelain sink. It was cracked where his right hand had been. He'd worn the edges of the crack down over the past thirty years, worrying about me and my sister, and now worrying about his nine-year-old granddaughter. My dad stood straight and shook his head.

—Then maybe it was just a routine revision? I said. He just stared at me. There was never anything routine about a revision.

—You going for a band? he asked. I nodded. It won't still be there.

—Maybe not a blue, but something else. Something with a bit more movement for Shelly.

His right hand passed over to the green band wrapped around his left wrist. He disagreed with my reasoning, but he didn't say anything.

—I'm going to get the truck ready, I said.

—Get more water, he said. Bring back some water.

—Yeah.

—You have enough gas?

I stopped at the door. My thumb punched the button on the screen door's handle a couple of times.

—There's probably a quarter tank, I said.

—You should get some more.

—Who's got any?

His hands resumed gripping the edge of the sink.

—I think around the corner, he said and looked up at me.

—Around the corner? I thought they stopped.

—They have a bit right now. Not sure where they got it.

—Okay. I'll stop there.

—Okay, he said. Here. He let go of the edge of the sink and opened the cupboard door above him.

—I have some, I said.

—Just take it.

He pushed aside a jar, pulled down the envelope, took two bills from it, and held them out to me.

—Is that all that's left in there? I asked.

He pulled the envelope apart to show me it was empty.

—Shoot, I said.

—Yeah.

—Just give me one.

—Take them both. Get as much as you can.

I took the two bills from my dad's hand and folded them into my back pocket.

—We'll be back later, I said.

—Yep.

My dad put his hands in the back pockets of his jeans.

I stepped out the front door onto the porch. Darkness still held the western horizon and the flares in the field across the street rose bright against the black backdrop. The oilrigs worked up and down. I could just make them out in the dark, their horseheads rotating high to low. They were louder this morning, more of them in motion, more of them whining through the slow oblong paths their spinning parts moved in. I walked across the brittle grass in the front yard.

I unlocked the door of the truck and opened it, then pulled the hood release and heard it pop open. The anode rotated back and forth until it cinched back tightly to the battery and I pulled out the spark plugs I'd put in the back pocket of my jeans last night and screwed them in. I brought the hood down and pushed it shut and walked back across the dry grass. I pulled the garage door open, grabbed the shovels and two chairs, and carried them to the truck. I went back in the house and Shelly was in the kitchen looking for something. She was on her toes at the sink, chatting with Grandpa.

—What's up? I asked her. What are you looking for?

—The water filter, she said.

—Do you have it? Dad asked me.

She bent down and pulled open the cabinet below the sink.

—It should be in there, I said.

—Here it is. She held the filter up for me and her grandpa to see.

—Great, I said. Where's the big water jug?

Shelly thought for a moment. The first of the morning sun, dusty and red, came through the window behind her.

—Garage, she said, her voice scratchy. She shut the cabinet and put the filter in her backpack.

—Shelly, you get some water yet? I asked.

She coughed and her chest took in a small breath and she coughed again. She nodded while she waited for her coughing to stop.

—Can you put some pants on? I asked her.

She shook her head. She zipped her backpack shut and twisted it over her shoulders to settle it snugly against her back. The hem of her yellow dress swayed left and right just above her red sneakers. She walked past me out the front door.

—These are my adventure clothes, she said, and she stepped down the front porch.

—What else do you have in your backpack?

—Adventure stuff, she said from the front yard, her voice louder now, less scratchy.

—You let her come out of her room like this? I said to my dad. He shrugged his shoulders.

I went into the garage and found the water container, and I grabbed two umbrellas and the cooler. I shut the garage door and took the items to the back of the truck. Shelly was at the passenger-side door waiting for me to open it. I threw her the keys.

—You feeling all right? I asked her.

She caught the key chain and flipped through to the key for the truck.

—Same, she said. She unlocked her door and threw the keys back to me. She undid her backpack from her shoulders with the same movements she'd used to get it on. Then she opened the door and threw the backpack onto the bench seat. She climbed in, and I closed the door behind her.

—Seat belt, I said through the glass.

—Doesn't work, she said.

—That's true.

The boy from the neighborhood watch was down the street a couple blocks, getting closer now. I got in the truck and rolled down the window. Shelly rolled down hers.

—You hear that? I said.

—Why is he still out?

—I don't know.

The boy's whistle blew again and we watched the watchman, the watchboy, ride his bike across the street left to right and then behind the houses on our side of the street.

—He'll come down the alley, right? Shelly said.

—Yeah.

Shelly followed the sound of the whistle as it came toward us from the alley on the other side of the houses. I did the same. Sunlight came from above the roofs of the houses across the street, and it lit up Shelly's face, tanned dark gold from the summer, and it streaked her black hair dark gold too.

—I wonder why he's still out? she asked.

The watchman was behind our house now. We saw him for a moment as he rode between our house and the neighbor's house, whistle in his mouth. Shelly tracked him a moment longer then turned and faced forward. She looked at me, and I shrugged my shoulders and told her I didn't know why he was still out past dark.

—I'm sure there's a good reason, she said. I nodded my head.

I put the key in the ignition and turned the engine on.

—It's pretty, Shelly said.

—What? I said, and pulled the truck into drive.

—The sunrise.

I looked left to where she was looking. The oilrigs to the east were hidden behind the houses, and the smoke from their flares held the morning glow of the sun and magnified it in size.

—Yeah, it's pretty, I said. Say bye to your grandpa.

My dad was leaning on the porch railing, his fingers flaking off chips of paint. Shelly gave him a couple of quick waves. He brought a hand up and waved back, and he didn't quite smile but did the best he could. His gray hair took on the red of the sunrise and the flares, recreating the reddish hair he had in pictures of him as a boy. I moved my foot from brake to accelerator and pulled right through the intersection where the watchman had gone. The kid was riding slowly, cutting his wheel left and right through the alley's gravel, blowing his whistle.

—I thought we were going to the reservoir, Shelly said, turning back to me.

—We are.

—It's that way, Shelly said and nodded back behind us, to the east, where we'd find the road north.

—We need gas.

—Oh.

I pulled to the curb at the next street. I put the truck in park.

—Doesn't look like anyone's home, Shelly said, staring through the intersection at the second house on the left. I turned the engine off, and we both stared at the house. The sole streetlamp on the block flickered out as more dull red light came over the horizon from the east. Should we go to a different gashouse? Shelly asked.

—Just a minute, I said.

The house before the gashouse, the one on the corner, had a broken chain-link fence around its yard, and a dog lay curled up next to its gate. The corners of the gate were no longer square; they'd been twisted somehow, squished, leaving an opening for the dog to come and go as it pleased. The gate's latch was still in place, though, grasping the pole still sunk in the ground, and the dog's nose rested below this latch on the concrete. Its eyes were closed.

The porch light of the gashouse turned on and off.

—You see that? my niece said.

—Yeah. I flashed my headlights twice and waited. The porch light flashed twice, and I started the truck. The dog's eyes opened and watched us turn left through the intersection. I pulled the truck into the alleyway, went past the dog's house, and stopped behind the gashouse. A man walked out the back door and stepped onto the small porch. It creaked and flexed under his mass. He waited there a moment. I shut off the engine. He looked up and down the alley and back at our truck. My hands were on top of the steering wheel, and I tipped them open to ask him what the wait was. He nodded his head and stepped down the two steps of the porch, each step flexing more than the porch had. He walked to Shelly's window.

—Hey, he said.

—You have gas?

He nodded his head. I gave him the two bills my dad had given me.

—How much do you want? he asked.

—How much does that buy?

He thought a moment.

—Ten, he said.

—That seems low.

He just kept looking at me. He shrugged his shoulders.

—Okay, I said. Where'd you get it?

—You want the ten? he asked.

—Yeah.

—Back into the garage, he said, and walked away without answering my question.

I started the truck and moved it forward, then backed toward the standalone shack that sat in the man's backyard. I braked as he hefted up the shack's door, then backed in. He closed the door. We were in darkness as he searched for the string hanging from the ceiling that was attached to a light bulb. He pulled on it when he found it and a dim bulb turned on and swung back and forth opposite the shadows on the walls. He walked to the gas cap and unscrewed it. His fuel tank was perched on two old refrigerators. He put the cap on top of the cab and pulled the hose from his tank to the truck and inserted the nozzle. He pulled the trigger and watched the meter on the handle spin as gravity brought the gas into the truck.

—When did you get more? I asked.

He stayed quiet.

—Are you back in?

He looked up briefly from the meter and shook his head.

—How'd you find gas?

—It's around. Not much. It's there if you ask the right people.

The walls of the shack were lined with shelves, and the shelves were lined with jugs of water and cans of food.

—Is that sweetwater? I asked.

—No. There hasn't been any sweetwater left for years. No matter who you ask. He snapped the gas off and slid the nozzle out of the truck.

—Go out the other end of the alley, he said.

—Okay, I said.

He turned the light off, and we sat in darkness again. Light came and went from behind us as he walked out a door. We listened to him walking to the front of the shack, his feet on the gravel of the alleyway. His footsteps stopped for a moment.

—It stinks in here, Shelly said.

—Yeah. Shh. Plug your nose.

His gravel footsteps started again, and as the door was opened, Shelly and I squinted at the light and I started the truck. We pulled past him and headed down the alley to the right. I stopped at the street and looked east, the sun was a little brighter now, up a little further. Two blocks east, then we'd go north. I looked back at my niece.

—You ready for adventure? I said to her.

—Ready, she said.

2   —Grab the umbrellas, I told her. Shelly slid from the seat onto the ground. She pulled the straps of her backpack onto her shoulders.

—Where are they? she asked.

I reached into the bed of the truck and pulled them out, one big, one small.

—Here, I said.

—Do we need both? She put her arms out and I handed her just the big one. I threw the small one back into the truck bed. She carried the umbrella in her arms like a stack of firewood.

—That'll help you balance through the muck.

—Like a trapeze artist, she said.

—That's right. I grabbed the cooler and the shovels and the two chairs.

—It's chilly out here, my niece said.

—Nice, right? Won't be chilly for long.

—Are we going to take our shoes off? She rolled her feet onto her ankles and back level again.

—You don't want to get those red shoes dirty.

—It's chilly though.

—Okay. We'll probably be all right for a while. You have to take them off when it gets gunky though.

—Yep.

She led the way down the path to where our footprints from yesterday started, cast in dry mud now like the others had been the day before, and she kept going until where the muck now started, and then stopped and tested the muck with a soft step.

—Seems okay, she said. Drier than yesterday.

—Great.

Shelly continued with careful steps farther out onto the reservoir floor. Her red shoes sank slightly. I followed in her short footsteps. She made a detour around a standing puddle then continued straight. The tread on her shoes was loose, and it stuck to the wet surface and then came free and slapped up against the soles of her feet when she stepped forward. Shelly exaggerated her steps now so that the treads slapped harder and she giggled at the pieces of muck flying out in front of her.

—Stop that, I said.

She giggled again and kicked a couple more times and then began to walk in her normal way.

—You're a good trail finder, I told her.

She glanced up and adjusted her route and kept leading us across the gray flats.

—The flares are really going today, she said.

I picked up my head for a moment. The large oilfield to the west was more full of flares than usual. More of the pumps were active.

—That's true, I said.

The flares rippled upward, ending where dark wisps of smoke began.

—They really smell today, Shelly said.

—More than usual?

—Yeah, she said.

We came to where the edge of the reservoir had been the day before. Our old footprints ended here, and the muck beyond this old shoreline was smooth and seamless. The bone Shelly had found lay tossed on the ground a few steps in front of us. The white liquid was recessed ten to fifteen yards farther. My niece started to say something but stopped and coughed and leaned forward and spat out a dark lump of phlegm that splattered over the pasty floor. She let the umbrella roll off her arms onto the ground and coughed again and held her hands to her stomach. I waited for the reverberations to pass through her body. The hem of her dress quivered and then stilled, and she dropped her hands to her sides and stood straight again. She composed herself, eyes closed, tried to get a fuller breath in but couldn't and let her breath out. Her chest rose again, trying to get more air in, but fell short and her shoulders slouched forward.

—Shoulders back, I said.

She arched them back and tried once more for more air, pulling it in slowly, and she got a little further but then hit a hitch and had to stop to let what air she had back out again.

—That's better, I said. Once more.

Her eyes opened and she wiped bloody mucous from her mouth and rubbed it onto the side of her dress, red on yellow. I waited for her to look at me.

—Once more, I said.

Shelly closed her eyes and arched her spine more fully now, taking her shoulders farther back, and started pulling air in again. Nearly full, she fought through a cough and tried to keep her lungs big for a moment and then let it out quickly and her rib cage and shoulders fell again and her upper body went limp.

—That's better, I said. Is that better?

She nodded and opened her eyes halfway and then the rest of the way and then tried to resume her natural standing position. I unfolded a chair and told her to sit down.

—I'm okay, she said.

—Well, there's a chair if you want to sit.

She nodded her head.

—I'm going to set up the umbrella, she said.

—Perfect. I handed her the shovel to dig a hole to sink the pole of the umbrella into.

Shelly stuck the point of the shovel into the chalky substrate and lifted one of her red tennis shoes onto it. She weighted her foot and the shovel sliced into the gunk. She threw a small shovelful of reservoir to her side and went for another one. I tried to smell the stench of the flares and their black smoke, but the rotten smell of the reservoir smothered it. I took in more air through my nose, trying to get a whiff, but nothing. Just muck. I bent over and picked up the broken ulnar bone. I flipped it aside. I took the other shovel and did as Shelly had done. I stepped the blade into the moist sediment of the reservoir floor until it wouldn't go any deeper, then lifted and threw the shovelful of sediment away from where the rest of the remains of the body lay below.

3   My niece stood up from her chair and came to the edge of the hole we'd dug and had a look at what we'd excavated so far. I stood in the hole, no deeper than the height of my knees, straddling the skeleton. The bones were still mostly covered in mud, glimpses of ribs showing through, a right angle from the hips to the femur, an acute turn from femur to tibia and fibula. I leaned out of the way so that Shelly could see it without obstruction. The bones had taken on the faint orange color of the clay substrate that lay beneath the surface. The skeleton was on its side, a little ball of a skeleton.

—It doesn't look very tall, Shelly said.

—Nope.

—How tall would it be on you? she asked.

I flipped the shovel upside down and hovered the end of the handle above the sole of the exposed foot and moved it up over the ankle and over its one visible tibia-fibula pairing and over the bend of the knee to its femur and pelvis and spine and petite rib cage and up to the top of the skull. I flipped the shovel back over and leaned on it and put my hand at the midway point of my chest. My niece nodded.

—Where am I on you?

I moved my hand down a bit to just above my hip. She nodded her head again.

—Stop chewing your hair, I said.

Shelly pulled the lock of hair from her mouth.

—Can you pump some water while I dig some more?

—Where's the filter? she asked.

—In the cooler. With the jug.

The arm with the missing ulna was on top and exposed, I could see it now. The arm was held close to the skeleton's chin. The arm's ragged end was no longer connected to its hand and its hand was nowhere in sight. Somebody had harvested the band already, when the skeleton was still a body, when the body was only recently deceased, or soon to be. I leaned the shovel against the side of the hole and wiped sweat from my forehead. I let out a sigh and leaned next to the shovel and looked up at Shelly, who was looking down past me to the bones.

—Are you going to keep digging? she asked.

I looked back down at the skeleton and nudged the handless forearm with the toe of my shoe. It came loose from its elbow and rolled to the bottom of the hole.

—I don't think so, I said.

Shelly moved to where her shadow fell over my face so that I didn't have an excuse not to look at her. I looked up and her eyes moved from mine to the bottom of the hole and back to mine again.

—Why not? she said.

—We should get the water and then get home, like Grandpa said.

—Then why did we come out here? she said. Come on. One more round of shovelfuls and we'd be able to lift it out. She moved her hand in an outline of the skeleton.

—Why are you so interested in this one? I asked her.

She walked to the cooler for the water filter.

—Can you throw me one of those candy bars in there? I asked her.

—Can I have one too?

—Of course.

She bent back to the cooler and grabbed two bars and lobbed one through the air to me. She put the pump and water jug down and unwrapped the bar and took a bite and picked up the filter and jug again and started walking to the water.

—Where's the water? she said, her back turned to me.

—Farther out, I guess.

Twenty yards from the hole she found the new edge of the reservoir and stopped.

—You're going to get your shoes all muddy, I said.

—That's okay. They're already muddy. She placed the jug on the reservoir floor and untangled the hoses of the filter and screwed the exit end to the jug and then readied the pump in her hands and let the entry end fall into the water. She bent nearer the ground and threw the end of the hose as far as it would go out into the water.

—The water's not very clear, she said. And it's not really deep enough.

—Just do the best you can.

—Okay.

The sound of her voice was small and thin, like it was barely making it across the distance between us. Her arms started working the handpump, her elbows moving out and in. She tucked the pump under her arm and fished her candy bar out of the chest pocket of her dress and took another bite, then replaced it and kept pumping while she chewed.

—Why are you so interested in this one? I asked her again. I threw another shovel of wet gunk out of the pit. She didn't answer until she had finished chewing and swallowing the bite of her candy bar.

—I want to find out who he is, she said.

—Was, Shelly. Who he was. He isn't *is* anymore.

—That doesn't make sense, she said.

—Is that your breakfast? I asked her.

—Maybe, she said. She glanced back at me and saw me lob another shovelful out of the hole. She stopped working the pump.

—You going to dig it up? she yelled, her lips stretched to one side.

—Maybe, I said.

—I knew it, she said, and giggled softly and turned back to her job with the water.

—You did not know it.

She nodded her head that she did.

—We won't be able to find out who he was, I said.

She ignored me.

After I made my way around the skeleton again, it was ready to be lifted. I tossed the shovel toward the pile of soggy dirt that had accumulated. The skull was cool to the touch, as was the damp reservoir bottom beneath it. Water had begun to pool in the pit. I ran my hands around the edge of the skeleton and threw out handfuls of muck. The smooth underside of the skull remained suctioned in place when I began lifting it. My other hand went underneath the tucked-up legs, and my plan was to hug all the bones together and hope they didn't fall apart.

—You're bringing it up already? my niece said.

I readjusted my grip.

—You get much water?

—Enough for a bit. She held up what looked like a quart sloshing around the jug.

I pulled the small pile of bones together and lifted it up and rested it on the edge of the hole. The skull detached from the spine as my hand came away.

—He's so small, Shelly said.

—She, I said.

—She? Shelly went from a crouch to kneeling.

—You're going to get your dress dirty.

She untucked the dress from beneath her knees and pulled it up off the ground.

—She? she said again.

—See how this part at the bottom of her pelvis is obtuse? The angle is wide?

She nodded her head, taking her eyes from the skull to where my fingers pointed.

—Get that hair out of your mouth.

She spat the lock out.

—You see it?

—Yeah, she said.

—That suggests she's female.

—A little girl.

—A teenager probably. Early teens.

Shelly carefully put a finger on the girl's broken arm and traced it to its ragged end.

—You've never seen a skeleton before? I asked.

—We've never dug one all the way up. We just leave them.

—True.

—I've seen bodies. Before they're skeletons. Never skeletons though.

—That's right, I said.

—Where's her band? she asked, her expression turning more serious.

—I couldn't find it.

Shelly rotated her yellow band around her wrist. It was tight and it was sweaty from working the water pump.

—Is that why you were interested in her?

—Maybe, I said. Sweat dropped from my forehead down the side of my nose and into my eyes, like it had the day before. My hands were too dirty to wipe it away today. It stung and blurred my vision and I kept my eyes closed, waiting for the stinging to go away.

—Here, Shelly said, and she ran her fingers down each side of my nose and past the corners of my eyes, expelling some of the sweat and tears there. I opened my eyes slowly and the yellow of Shelly's dress was bright and foggy and I closed my eyes tightly again and passed my upper arms over both of them and waited a moment more. I opened one eye, the one I thought was now clear. The sun was halfway up into the sky; its brightness burned away any chill that the morning had left. I closed both eyes again and turned from the white glare. I passed my mud-caked hands over my T-shirt to clean them.

—And now? Shelly asked. Are you interested in her now?

—I'm not sure, I said. I cracked my eyes open and things were more focused and Shelly's yellow dress not so blurry and not so bright. I brushed my hands together and pushed them over the thighs of my pants.

—So what now? she said.

My hands were almost dry and the remaining mud cracked and drifted to the ground in curtains of dust as I pushed and twisted my palms against each other.

There was trouble east of Conrad. My sister had reported that. We were directly north of wherever the trouble was. Dad thought there was a change going on. He was anxious. The route home would be southwest. West first, then south.

—We pack her up and take her to the truck, I said, and I pushed myself up out of the shallow grave.

—And then what?

—I don't know, Shelly. Let's get to the truck first.

Shelly brought the cooler over to the skeleton.

—Is there anything in there? I said.

—Two more candy bars. And a flashlight.

—Okay, take those out.

—Why is there a flashlight in the cooler? Shelly asked.

—Good question.

She grabbed the candy bars and flashlight and held them out in front of her.

—Put them in your backpack.

She turned and found her backpack.

I leaned onto my knees and slipped my hands under the skeleton, as I had done to lift it from the pit. The skull stayed on the ground. The rest of the bones minus a couple of metatarsals from her feet stayed connected and I lifted her into the cooler. As I brought my arms out from underneath her, more bones detached and settled out individually. Her broken skeleton lay on the bottom of the cooler. The bones that remained together did so only because of the red reservoir mud that clung to them. I picked up the bones that had fallen on the ground and put them with the others. The skull stayed there in the muck; Shelly bent over and picked it up.

—Careful with the jaw. It might come undone. Where's the filter?

—In my backpack.

—You have everything in that backpack.

She nodded.

The shovels and the lawn chairs and the umbrella didn't take long to round up and I gave the umbrella to Shelly so she could carry it again like a tightrope walker and I threaded the lawn chairs up onto my shoulder and carried the shovels together in one hand. With the other hand I grabbed the rope connected to the handle of the cooler and put the water jug in this hand too and began dragging the cooler full of bones.

—Ready to go? I said to Shelly. She skipped once to better situate her backpack on her shoulders and tucked the skull underneath her arm and held the umbrella flat across on the undersides of her forearms. Her muddied red tennis shoes started for the parking lot.

—What color do you think her band was? my niece asked.

Strands of black hair were plastered with sweat over her forehead and down over her eyes. I told her to wait a second and she stopped. I put the rope and cooler down and pulled her hair from her face and tried to tuck it behind her ear. It fell back over her eyes. I tried to help her again, but she said it was fine.

—Can you see? I asked her. She shrugged.

There were no mirages surrounding us today. It wasn't quite afternoon yet.

—What time is it? I asked her.

—My watch is in my backpack. She started walking again.

Smoke from the flares streamed in straight, thin lines into the sky. The flames weren't that noticeable now, the sunlight bleaching them away. Then the black lines of smoke dissipated into the brown horizon, and then up into the haze of white in the sky above that.

—Will the people say anything about the skeleton? Shelly asked.

—At the roadblocks?

—Yeah.

—I don't know. I doubt it, I said.

I stopped and put the shovels and lawn chairs on the other side of my body and switched the rope on the cooler and the water jug to my other hand. Shelly kept walking, her head down, putting one foot directly in front of the other, her eyes still steady on the imaginary rope in front of her, a curtain of hair down over her eyes.

—Look up at the horizon, I told her.

—Really?

—Yeah.

—That's how they do it?

—Yeah. They're looking for a point that doesn't move. It helps them balance better.

—I'll look at the truck, she said. She flicked her head back to clear some of her hair out of the way and it seemed to help.

—What are you walking over?

—It's a big canyon.

—With a river at the bottom?

—Yeah, a big river.

—Lucky there's no wind, I said. Don't look down.

She nodded then shook her head and took a few more linear steps on her rope, toe-to-heel, toe-to-heel, and then walked normally again, letting the rope and canyon and river all disappear.

—I bet they don't say anything, she said.

—Who?

—The people who search through all the stuff at the points of revision.

—About the bones?

—Yeah.

—You might be right.

—I'm hot, she said.

—We'll drink some of that water you pumped when we get to the truck.

—It's so gross, she said.

—I know. It tastes bad.

It looked like she was going to get back on her tightrope again, but she started coughing and she stopped walking altogether. I stopped too. She worked her way through a couple lungfuls of coughs and got her regular breath back. I asked her if she was all right and she didn't say anything, just kept her eyes closed for a bit and stood still, her chin against her chest. She looked up and found the truck, a consistent point on the horizon, something to steady her coughing, and started walking again.

4 We got to the parking lot and the cooler's bottom side scraped across the cracked asphalt. Shelly took two tightrope steps on a dim yellow line that had once marked parking spots and made her way to the bed of the truck and threw the umbrella in.

—Gently, I said.

She moved the skull from its pinched position between her arm and side and held it in both hands.

—Here, I said, and handed her the jug of water. She walked to the hood and stood on her tippy toes to put the skull on it and steadied it there for a moment, making sure it didn't start to roll or slide. Then she came back for the jug and twisted the valve on the cap and pushed it above her head and a stream of foggy water splashed off her cheek until she aimed it into her mouth.

—Don't waste it, I said. Her cheeks bellowed out and she brought the jug down and handed it to me while she swallowed the water, her eyes squinting, fighting back the sulfur taste.

—Thanks. I took water into my mouth and tried to swallow it but the sulfur water wouldn't go down. I began to gag and tried again but my throat wouldn't open. I spat the water onto the asphalt.

—Hey! Shelly said. You said not to waste.

—How'd you do that? I asked her.

—I was thirsty, she said.

—It's so bad. I wiped the drips of water from my face and took the keys out of my pants and opened the door of the truck. Shelly popped it open and threw her backpack in. I put the cooler and the shovels and the lawn chairs in the bed of the truck.

I drove the truck slowly over the potholed asphalt of the reservoir parking lot. Shelly held the girl's skull in her lap, dust falling into the yellow folds of her dress. She pinned it between her knees and rotated her band around her wrist.

—My band's tight, she said.

—They're not meant to be loose, I told her.

—But it's too tight.

—We'll take you in and get it adjusted.

—I like the yellow, she said, and turned it around her wrist one more time and then stopped fiddling with it.

—Yellow's a good color, I told her. It's good you like it.

—That's what everyone says.

She lifted the skull from her lap and put it between us on the bench seat. Her forearm rested on it. I stopped the truck at the parking lot exit. The sun was almost above us, the morning mostly through.

—We going home now? she asked. We looked right and left. Right was north and away from home; left was south and toward home. We'd have to go south the shortest distance possible and then a quick west to avoid whatever my sister had seen and then south again. I ran this through my brain, putting one unknown with other unknowns and adding the general warnings of my sister and calculating what might result. Home would work. We'd go home. I took my foot from the brake, looking south, but Shelly told me to wait. I stepped on the brake again and looked to where she was pointing: north. A line of vehicles had come over a rise not far off and were traveling fast, heading south.

—A force line, she said.

The front car had its roof lights going, a swirl of green and yellow. Trucks followed close behind. I reversed from the intersection. The high hum of tires got louder. Men and women in masks sat atop the vehicles, some standing up through sunroofs, others standing on the beds of trucks and leaning forward onto the cabs in front of them. Long guns were slung over the backs of their shoulders. The lead car passed us and the line of vehicles came in quick succession after that, each vehicle's sound running past us, loud and quick, followed by a light shower of pebbles that rolled and bounced up against Shelly's side of the truck. The men and women, with their masks and goggles on, tracked us as they moved past, their T-shirts and shorts flapping in tight waves around their bodies. The mini-hailstorm of pebbles continued pelting the side of our truck after the last vehicle passed us. Two people sat on the open tailgate, kicking their feet in the wind. One waved as they rushed away. A solitary pebble bounced off our windshield and onto the hood of our truck and spun in a nearly perfect rotation around its north-south axis before it started to wobble and then toppled and lay still.

—Whoa. Did you see that? Shelly said. She was looking at the pebble on the hood.

—Yeah, I said. We took our eyes slowly from the pebble and looked left, at the trucks driving away from us. The hum of their tires was almost gone, and the men and women with their masks and their long guns were off in the distance, disappearing south down the highway. Shelly tracked them with her hand up to her forehead, guarding against the glare from the cracks in the windshield. She tracked them until the last truck, with the two people on the tailgate, passed from view. She dropped her hand from her forehead and let out a breath she must have been holding for a while. Her lungs filled slowly again, stopped when she could pull no more air in, and then collapsed downward, her shoulders slouching. Her eyes went from where the last truck had disappeared from sight up to me.

—Left still? she said.

—No.

We drove in the opposite direction from the line of enforcer vehicles. Wind came through the windows and it felt good to be in moving air again, the heat of the day having arrived. The pebble that had landed on the hood was vibrating with the movement of the truck now, sliding slowly to the side. Both Shelly and I kept an eye on it until it fell off her side of the hood. We refocused on the road ahead.

The flares coming from the oilrigs in the fields that we drove past emitted small specks of black, which we drove through. They hit the windshield in a dim clatter and blew through our windows and we breathed in these pieces of grit and we pushed them around our mouths until we had to spit them out. The flares closest to the road radiated heat off the side of the truck and through our windows and up against the sides of our faces. Shelly's hair blew across her face and she left it there.

—The flares are pretty, my niece said. I looked over at the flares Shelly was watching. She followed one past her window and then looked up ahead and tracked another.

—Yeah, they are, I said.

She watched the horseheads on the oilpumps work up and down. We drove past one herd of them and went down another draw, and the next herd covered the gradual bluff in front of us. Three-quarters of them spun, the others stood in various still-life positions, looking to the sky or grazing with their noses to the ground. Ahead, a line of water trucks came over the bluff and passed us and more rocks snapped against our truck and up across our windshield. Shelly and I flinched at a big one that left a dime-sized star in the windshield, joining the others in their constellations.

—When did my mom leave this morning?

—I'm not sure. Maybe around four.

Another rock cracked against the grille of our truck and Shelly jumped a bit in her seat and then all the water rigs were behind us, leaving only a few remnant gusts blowing through our open windows, lifting and fluttering loose papers and pieces of refuse at our feet.

—When do you go back to work? she asked.

—No work this year, I said.

She leaned forward and put her index finger on the new star in the windshield. She leaned back with a slight bounce and exhaled.

—That's a big one, she said, squinting at the shine of the new star. She kept her eyes on it.

I looked over and tried to see what she was seeing. She leaned forward again and traced her finger from star to star, drawing over the constellations that had been there for a while, and then she bent one of the connecting lines to incorporate the new star, then she continued. She sat back again.

—Any new constellations? I asked.

—Not sure yet, she said. I didn't hear her leave, she said, still looking at the stars. She swiped sweat from her forehead with the back of her hand and looked again at the oil derricks passing.

—She doesn't like to wake you. She's good at sneaking out. I'm sure she said goodbye to you.

—Yeah, she said. But there was trouble this morning? She fluffed some of the dirt off her dress that had fallen from the skull and it swept up into the breezes passing through the cab and flew in front of our eyes.

—Wait until we're out of the car to do that, I said.

—Okay, she said. That's what Grandpa was talking about?

—This morning? Yeah. How much did you hear?

She shrugged.

Another four-way stop neared and I slowed the truck and let it coast before pushing the brake again. On the side of the road, two men had a blue tarp strung from the side of a defunct oilrig and the tarp's ends were staked to the ground. A small table sat in the shade of the tarp and the men were at either end of the table playing cards. Their guns leaned up against the table and both the men tilted back their chairs, the front feet held in the air. One man leaned forward and put his chair on all fours and he laid down a card. The other man threw his cards in and a conversation ensued. They didn't register our presence with anything more than a glance. The losing man collected the cards and began to shuffle them as I took the truck through the intersection.

—Why no work? Shelly asked.

—What do you mean?

—You said no work this year.

—No school, I said.

She pressed the creases out of her dress, her palms pressing into her knees, then let the tension out and the creases came back, then she pressed them away again, then let them return. She kept up this fidgeting until she thought of what to say.

—How's that? she said.

—Last year was the last year.

—So how are your students going to learn biology? she said.

—Not sure.

Her left arm rested on the skull again.

—Wait, she said, rubbing the skull's right temple and flaking off thin layers of dirt. What about me?

—No school. I steered the truck around a pothole. Shelly swayed back and forth and then settled again.

—No school, she said.

—Nope.

Her head turned to the land passing by the side of the car, slightly tilted telephone poles holding thin wires, a dry stream filled with brown sand, bare ground with a few weeds scattered between oilrigs. There was a rusted-out wheat combine, unused for decades. And up ahead a hay bale conveyor tipped on its side, its belt gone. These and other farm instruments were half-buried in drifts of sand and dust, sinking into the bedrock lying beneath them, dust blown off of one instrument landing quickly on another.

—So what are we going to do? she said.

—We're going to find out who this girl is.

—Even without her band?

—You said we can, I said. Shelly looked up from staring at the smooth temple of the skull.

—Yeah, we can, she said.

—Okay, I said. Then we can.

My niece pulled the skull back on her lap and moved her thumb to the other temple. Wisps of dust flew through the cab again.

—Hey, I said, waving the dust away from my face.

—Sorry.

—That sound good? I asked.

She coughed and nodded at the same time.

—Cover your mouth.

—Sorry, she said.

—Okay, I said, and kept the truck heading north, trying to think how we would make it back south. Shelly leaned forward again and touched the newest star in the windshield.

—Now our Big Dipper has a North Star to point to, she said, having solved how the new star fit in with the rest, and traced her finger down from the new star to the two stars on the side of the Dipper. The glass was full of pockmarks. She ran her finger back up to the new North Star and rotated her elbow away so she could look for stars that might make the Little Dipper. She moved her elbow the other way and looked some more and then let her finger slip from the windshield and her hand dropped back to her lap. I leaned over and took a look.

—Yep. You're right, I said. Now we got to wait for the Little Dipper to appear.

She nodded her head and squinted at all the splintering light coming through the glass.

—Your phone's ringing, Shelly said.

—I don't think I brought my phone, I said.

—Yeah you did. I brought it.

—Good thinking.

Shelly brought her backpack from where it sat by her feet up to her lap. She unzipped its main compartment and started digging around. Her hand came up out of the bag with the phone. She turned it right side up.

—Who is it?

—It's Grandpa, she said.

She looked at me while it rang in her hand again.

—See what he wants, I told her.

Her thumb found the phone's edge and flipped it open.

—Hey, Grandpa, she said, and rolled her window up. Her hair stopped knotting and unknotting itself in the wind and fell around her shoulders. She took the phone away from her ear for a moment to tuck her hair away from her face and then put the phone back up to listen.

—We're back in the truck, she said. We're on a highway. Heading north.

She cracked her window a bit.

—Yeah, we have the skeleton in the back of the truck, she said. She sat straight and strained her neck to the slit in the window where air came into the car. The heat in the car was building fast.

—He's a girl, Grandpa. Her eyes were closed and she drew in a long breath of air while she listened to my dad. She slouched back against the seat again.

—What's he saying? I asked.

Shelly waved me off. She listened. She took her window all the way up again and leaned into the phone to listen more closely. I rolled up my window so she could hear better. I heard her say yes and no and uh-huh.

—He says we should head home.

—Tell him about the line of enforcers.

She told my dad about the line of trucks we'd seen and then listened until my dad had said everything he needed to and then she said she loved him too and snapped the phone shut and put it where she had found it in her backpack. Her hand went to the window crank and she opened it all the way. I did the same. Her hair returned to knotting and unknotting itself around her head.

—Grandpa said we're heading to the aqueduct.

—Yep.

She put her hands on the skull again and lifted it back on her lap. She began flaking more crusted dirt off but then remembered and stopped.

—What else did he say I was going to do? I asked.

—She had a cavity.

—What?

—Look, she said. Shelly had the skull tilted onto the back of its head and she was looking into her mouth, letting the jaw drop open.

—Here, she said, pointing to a molar.

I leaned over and there it was, a metal cap covering the top of a tooth.

—You're right, I said.

—Is it gold? she asked.

—It could be. Probably not.

She looked more closely.

—What else? I said.

—What else what?

—What else did Grandpa say? Anything about getting home?

She brought the jaw back up carefully to close the mouth and turned the unknown girl's head around again so it faced forward.

—He said your girlfriend's out there.

—He did not say that, I said.

—Well, no, not exactly, but Mom told him and then Grandpa said it to me.

—What was your mom doing home already?

—I don't know. I didn't ask.

—How much does your mom tell you about this stuff? I said.

—What stuff?

—Girlfriend stuff. My girlfriend stuff.

—Not much, Shelly said.

—Too much, I said.

—Not that much.

—And she's not my girlfriend. That ended a long time ago.

—You shouldn't get mad.

—She's my ex. And I'm not mad.

—She said you'd say that.

—What? That I'd say which?

—Both.

—Hmm.

I regripped the steering wheel and sat up in my seat and readjusted the rearview mirror, which the potholes had knocked out of place. Shelly patted the skull on the brim of its forehead.

—Your mom's pretty smart, I said.

—Yeah, she said.

—She say anything else?

Shelly pulled her backpack between her feet and unzipped the front pocket and fished for something.

—Shelly?

She turned her head toward her window, her hand still searching for something. I leaned forward and she was hiding a smile.

—Shelly! I said.

—What? she said.

—What else?

—She said not to call Jen your girlfriend.

—What?

Shelly pulled her hand from the backpack and she plopped back in her seat and she giggled quietly. I shook my head and she started to giggle again.

—Shelly, I said.

—Don't get mad, she said.

—Is that your mom telling me not to get mad or you telling me not to get mad?

She laughed again. Both, she said, and bounced up against the backrest of her seat, her hair bouncing over her face.

—Shelly, I said, and looked up the road. Now you're the smart one.

—Yep.

5   We pulled up to an intersection, and to the west there should have been mountains, but they were far away and they were cloaked with the same haze that covered the land in each direction. I leaned forward and looked up through the windshield to see if there were any clouds. There weren't. Just white sky dulled at its edges to an off-white color before it turned brown at the horizons that stretched around us, flat and unbroken, no buildings or silos or mountains or anything. My niece flapped her hands in front of her face to cool the sweat.

—Left? she said.

—Yeah, west, I said. I didn't move the truck. Hey, when you were talking with your grandpa, did he say why your mom was home early from work?

Shelly shook her head.

—But your mom got through the points of revision fine on the way back?

Shelly nodded her head and shrugged.

—What else did he say?

—He said the aqueduct or home. Those are our only options.

—Yeah. Anything else?

—He said he loves you.

—Yeah, I said. I love him too.

—Yep. Shelly rested her hands on her lap and we sat in the still air with heat pushing down on us. Aqueduct or home.

—Did he say which way home?

She shook her head.

—He said you'd know though.

—Yeah. That meant east. Way east. Deep into the plains. Then far south. And back west again.

—Is it going to keep getting hotter? she asked, looking at me and then past me to the west.

—Yeah, I said.

—It's going to get so hot, she said.

—Yeah.

I pulled left through the intersection, west. The air coming in the window felt cool again for a moment. Shelly smiled through this moment, and then pulled the skull into her belly and began coughing, her smile wiped away. She coughed through a lungful of air and ended up arched over the skull in a quiet slouch. I put my hand over her back.

—You okay?

She moved her bowed head in slow affirmation.

—Cover your mouth, I said.

She made the same affirmative movement with her head.

—Okay, I said.

All our windows were fully open now, and we both put our arms on our windowsills and air whipped in and over us and then out the cab window behind us. My niece rested her head on her arm, leaning it halfway out the window, and wind bent her hair in dark locks and pulled it wildly up and down, making her squint her eyes. In the expanse ahead of us, there were fields of oilrigs and fields of brown and fields of blowing dust devils, throwing the unrooted dirt up into the air. Out in one of these fields, a girl of Shelly's age walked with a handheld radio that swung from her wrist. She had short hair and wore jeans that didn't reach her ankles. Her hair was lighter than Shelly's, almost blond, and the hand that wasn't swinging the small AM/FM radio was sunk deep down in the bottom of her pants pocket. The path she took was straight, similar to ours in direction, although her eyes weren't looking ahead at where she might be going. She looked down, maybe at her shadow, which would have been falling only inches in front of her, only inches farther north than where she was. This girl with the short blue jeans and bright hair moved slowly from in front of us, out there in that field walking between all those oilpumps, to our side, where I tried to keep an eye on her while keeping us on the road, until she was behind us and I stopped trying to track her through the open cab window. I lost her behind a rig. I turned on the truck's radio and spun through the call numbers to see if there were any stations out here, to see if I might catch what the girl was listening to, but the dial just kept running through the stations without stopping. I shut it off.

In ten minutes I slowed for a bridge that was approaching and pulled as far to the right on the bridge as I could. I asked my niece how much water was down there below the bridge.

—Water? she said.

—Yeah. We need water. It might taste better here from the river.

—There's no water here.

—Really?

She kicked herself higher in her seat and took another look.

—Nope. She slid back down with a plop on her seat.

I looked back through the cab window, back where the girl had been walking, but there'd be no chance of seeing her. She was far behind us now.

—What are you looking for? Shelly said.

—Nothing, I said.

—Is there supposed to be water here?

—Well, not really. Not this time of year. There was a chance though. I thought maybe we'd get lucky.

I let off the brake and the truck crept forward. I glanced backward again and a dust devil grew up from the side of the road and moved onto the far end of the bridge. It spun and moved dry, broken leaves in half circles over the potholed asphalt and sputtered out and disappeared before the dim double yellow line.

—Was there ever water here this time of year? Shelly asked.

—Yep.

I pushed the accelerator and got us moving toward where the highway, the river, and the road all intersected.

—Why'd the water stop?

—No more trees, I said.

—Trees here? Doesn't seem like there'd ever be trees out here.

—Not here. Up in the mountains.

—What would trees up there in the mountains have to do with water down here?

—Trees kept the water for later. You know how sometimes we save water for later? Even if we're thirsty now?

—Like we're saving that stinky water?

—Yeah.

—I guess. Yeah.

—That's what the trees did. Except the water didn't stink.

She tapped the skull on its forehead, letting the fingers on both her hands fall onto it in quick succession, from pinky to pointer. She did this with her fingers when she was thinking.

—So no trees, no water saving for later, she said.

—That's right.

—Where'd they save it?

—In the soil, up by their roots.

—And it slowly leaked out throughout the summer.

—You got it.

—There it is, she said.

—What.

—The aqueduct.

—Oh yeah. Good eyes.

The river passed under the highway up ahead first, then under the road we were on. The three of them didn't quite intersect. I pulled up underneath a solitary cottonwood that stood dead and leaning over the aqueduct. Its bifurcating trunk and thick branches threw down a small web of shade and when I stopped beneath this shadow, a dark swath of shade covered our windshield. My niece threaded her hands together and pushed her palms out in front of her and stretched and yawned.

—There it is, she said, looking out her window at the aqueduct.

It stretched west without a flinch, straight and flat. A scribble of water sat in its floor, meandering left and right between the concrete inclines that guided the water east to the reservoir. Shelly pulled her feet up on the seat and sat on them to get a better look at the cement river.

—You see her? my niece asked.

I pushed myself up to look over Shelly.

—I don't see her, I said, and let myself back down.

—I don't see her either, she said.

—Nope.

—But you can't really see much of the aqueduct from here, actually.

—Nope.

Shelly popped her door open and slid down to the ground. She turned around, brushing her yellow dress flat against her knees.

—You coming? she said.

—Get your hat on, I told her.

She stepped to the truck and opened her backpack and brought out a red baseball cap and pulled it on, adjusting it around her head, and grouped her hair in back so that it fit better or felt more comfortable, and zipped her backpack up.

—It matches your shoes, I said.

—Yep. You coming?

—Yeah. I'm coming. Lock your door. I pulled the lever to pop the hood and got out. I propped the hood open, unhooked the battery, and took off the distributor cap.

—Here, my niece said, and opened her backpack for me to place the cap in and she zipped it shut and threaded her arms through the straps. I brought the hood down and let it fall shut. The clamor of metal on metal dispersed without recoil through the empty flatness around us. Shelly coughed and this sound too dispersed without an echo. She hooked her thumbs through the straps of her backpack. Her head bent forward and she spat a dark piece of phlegm onto the road and wiped her forearm across her face and righted herself.

—You coming? she said.

—You keep asking that.

She pulled a loose strand of hair from her face and tucked it behind her ear and under her ball cap. She kept her eyes on me.

—Of course I'm coming, I told her.

6   Shelly kicked her leg over the rail and straddled it with her dress in an upside-down V. She paused for a moment, waiting until I was at the guardrail, then brought her second leg over and patted her dress flat and leaned on the rail, looking down into the aqueduct.

—The walls are steep, she said.

—Yeah.

She pushed herself off the guardrail and put a first foot on the decline.

—Careful, I said.

She put her second foot on the decline, her knees bent slightly, her toes pointing down, and took another step.

—Go down on a diagonal, I said to her, but gravity had already taken her to her fourth step and then her fifth until she couldn't fight it anymore. The pitter-patter of her strides quickened and the weight of the backpack pushed her chest forward and her speed increased and so did the relative possibility of catastrophe. She met the bottom of the aqueduct and her waist folded forward but she succeeded in putting a couple of long strides ahead of her and she broke most of her momentum until she fell onto her side and rolled once. I stepped over the barrier and waited to see how she'd recover. She was facedown, backpack up riding on her shoulders, palms to the concrete floor of the river in a push-up position. She turned her head to the side, then toward me at the guardrail. I took two steps to the edge of the decline.

—Thumbs up? I said.

She laid her cheek to the concrete.

—I'm coming down. I took a shallower descent than she had. Halfway down I noticed she had rolled over and was sitting up, wiping aqueduct dust off her elbows. I made it to the bottom and walked over to her. She raised her hand and I took it and pulled her to her feet. She shushed her dress back and forth, more dust falling off of her.

—Any scrapes? I asked.

She showed me the abrasions on her palms. I pressed my thumbs where there weren't any and kneeled down and brought her hands closer to me. I brushed a few more pebbles from each one.

—Good catch, I said. She nodded.

—Good adventure, she said, trying to calm herself. She took as deep a breath as she could, moving the air carefully over the hitches in her lungs, then exhaled slowly and quietly.

—I'm glad you didn't roll through the river, I said. A strip of flat, milky water ran a few feet from where she'd come to rest. The foggy water ended a handful of steps farther downstream, with no more water to push it down the nearly flat riverbed.

—True, she said.

—No blood?

—Nope. Just scrapes.

—Okay.

She had another look at her elbows and pulled the hem of her dress above her knees to examine them and then let her dress fall.

—Nope, she said again.

—Ready?

Shelly looked at the end of the strip of flat water near where she had come to a stop.

—The river just stops right there, she said.

I looked upstream at the ribbon of water that lay there moving nowhere. Downstream the aqueduct was dry and empty. The concrete inclines concentrated all the sun's rays and focused them right on us. The day was hot.

—Ready? I asked.

—Yeah.

She readjusted her red ball cap and hopped her backpack into a better place on her shoulders and we started walking upstream, although it was hard to tell if it was really upstream. We walked toward where the mountains were hiding behind the brown air on the horizon and that made the direction we walked upstream rather than downstream. We came to our first chance to cross the thin ribbon of murky water and my niece pulled her dress up over the tops of her red tennis shoes as she readied to step into and out of it. With two steps she was through, the water not even having crested her rubber soles, and she stomped her feet out on the dry concrete. She turned to see what kind of footprints she'd left.

—When was the last time there were trees? she asked, turning back around and walking up the aqueduct. Her head was down, watching the toes of her shoes poke out from under her dress with each step she took, watching the treads flap against the soles of her feet and flick specks of water in front of her until there was no more water to flick.

—Well, there are patches of trees left.

—But when was there lots? she said.

A small rock lay on the concrete riverbed in front of me and I kicked it and it bounced along the bed, hopping once through the next ribbon of river, and then it bounced once or twice up the southern bank's incline until it came to rest again on the concrete bottom. It hadn't made any sound as it hopped. All its sound had vanished somewhere between where it bounced and where we walked.

—You turn ten in September? I asked her.

—Yep. She skipped a little as she said this.

—So there were still trees up in the mountains two years before you were born.

—That's a long time ago.

—Yeah. Well, no. Not that long ago. Does it feel like a long time ago for you?

—I've known you for a long time, she said.

—That's true. All your life.

—Yep.

She walked to the same rock I had kicked and kicked it, her loose tread rolling back under her foot, and the rock spun and hopped like it had when I had kicked it, and it did make a sound each time it skipped off the concrete—I had been mistaken—it just seemed like there should have been more sound. Shelly stopped to watch the last few rolls and bounces of the stone.

—Does that sound right to you? I asked her.

—It sounds hollow, she said.

I nodded my head. That was right. It sounded hollow. I curved my stride toward where it had come to rest. The hood of the truck had sounded the same way when I had closed it.

—It feels like a long time ago, she said.

—Since we had trees in the mountains?

—Yeah, she said.

—Yeah, I said. I think you're right.

I was a couple of strides from the stone again.

—Really kick it hard this time, my niece said. So it sounds like something.

I took a crow hop and aimed diagonally across the bed so we could see it climb the incline a bit. I swung my toes at it and the point of my tennis shoe sent the pebble skimming over the concrete. We both stood still to watch and listen to it more closely. It hopped up onto the incline and arched to its apex and then made its way back down to the bed and tumbled to a stop.

—Did you hear it that time? I asked Shelly.

—Yeah, she said. But I almost didn't, she added.

—Exactly, I said. It's so weird.

—Yeah, Shelly said.

We continued walking, noticing how our footsteps didn't make much noise either, as if we were walking in a huge enclosed theater where all echoes and reverberations had been canceled out.

—You've never been down here? my niece asked. She brought her elbow up to reexamine one of her scrapes. She blew on it and rubbed it gently and then let it fall to her side.

—Only when there was water in it, I said. And no concrete.

—What do you mean, no concrete?

—When it was a regular river, just rocks and mud and plants in it.

—And that was a long time ago too, right? she asked.

—Even longer, I said.

—There's one of her drawings, Shelly said.

—Where?

Shelly pointed upstream and to the right, not far from where the stone had stopped rolling.

—Oh yeah, I said.

I'd never seen the drawings. They were paintings. Or spray paintings. I wasn't really sure. I knew my ex hadn't liked to hear them called drawings. She'd been out here making them for five years.

—Stephany, my niece said, reading the first name spray-painted on the incline. Each letter of *Stephany* was yellow and had thick black borders. The border of each letter lay over the one that followed it. Other names piled above and below this one, reaching the top of the incline and down to the bottom, where the bed of the aqueduct sat. Each name had its own color, blending or contrasting with the names that surrounded it. We squinted at the brightness the sun reflected off each letter.

—It's pretty, my niece said. She put her hand up to her forehead to block the glare as she had at the reservoir. It couldn't have helped much. Her eyes were nearly closed trying to fight back the light.

—Did you know her? Shelly asked.

—Stephany? I think so, yeah, I said. So did you.

—I did?

—Yeah. You remember the woman who was always outside the gas station? Hanging out by the street?

—The one who cleaned windshields?

—That one, I said.

—The one with the really blond hair.

—That's her, I said.

—What did someone want with her? she asked.

I shrugged.

The names stretched on to the west until one couldn't be distinguished from the other and all that was visible after this point was a wall of carefully painted colors reaching out into the distance until even these colors could no longer distinguish themselves from one another and they all blended into a color that had no name, like the color below the brown that covered the lower portion of the sky. This color with no name began again on the left side, the southern incline, and ran along this wall as it did on the northern one until the nameless color began separating itself into colors with names and then eventually the colors separated themselves enough to be distinguished as names of people. The southern names stopped twenty yards from where my niece and I stood.

—What's the first one over there say? my niece asked, her eyes straining.

—Where are your glasses?

She tapped the bottom of her backpack.

We continued west and stopped in front of the first name on the southern incline.

—Edward, Shelly said.

—Yep.

These names were painted with angular letters, in contrast to the northern wall's smooth corners. The colors were different too, not as primary as the northern ones, more born of mixtures, one not quite red, another not quite blue.

—These are pretty too, my niece said.

—Yeah, they are.

—She's a good drawer, she said.

—Yeah, she is. Don't call her that though. She likes to be called a painter.

—Okay. Painter.

My niece looked west down the aqueduct and then leaned around me to look east, where the aqueduct was still its barren color of gray.

—Where is she? she asked.

—I'm not sure.

—Is she usually here by now? she said.

—I don't know.

Shelly squinted at Edward's name, even though his name was darker, not quite maroon, easier to look at even with the sun glaring down.

—Did you know Edward? she asked me.

—No. I didn't know Edward. Did you?

She thought for a bit.

—I don't think so, she said. Shelly moved her tongue side to side over her teeth, maybe picking a stray piece of candy bar from her gums, maybe trying to spread some moisture around her mouth.

—Thirsty? I asked.

—Yeah.

—Me too.

A drop of sweat ran into my eye and I blinked it out, wiping it off my cheek.

—Do you want to go sit in the shade? I asked.

She didn't answer right away. She looked west, to where shade lay beneath the overpass of the highway. She looked back at Edward's name.

—Yeah, I'm hot, she said.

—Me too.

Shelly whispered the names spelled out in the paintings as we walked toward the mountaintops that sat somewhere west. They were painted in large letters, and Shelly's head swiveled left to right when she read each name, and she looked from north to south and back again, trying to read them all.

—There's too many, she said.

—There are.

She kicked another small stone and it ran away from us, rattling off its hollow sounds, and settled in the riffleless water of the river.

—Let's get to the shade, I said.

She nodded once and slouched a bit, walking slowly now, the heat sinking in all around us. A few other pebbles lay on the concrete riverbed, but we ignored them all.

7   Shelly dropped her backpack and sat down on the concrete. She rested her back against the incline.

—It's cold, she said, pausing, then slowly reclined her head until it also lay against the incline. I sat a few feet away from her.

—You okay? I asked.

She didn't answer, just breathed slowly in and out, acclimating to the coolness pressing into her back.

—So what happens to my friends? she asked. Her eyes closed and her hands pressed, palms down, against the cold aqueduct floor. She swallowed hard, pushing phlegm down her throat.

—You should spit that out, I said.

—I don't want to cough right now.

—Okay.

—My friends? she said.

—I don't know.

She coughed a small cough, not able to ignore it, and her back arched and bounced slightly against the incline.

—Depends on their parents.

—Okay, she said, then if you were a parent and your kid didn't have a school to go to next year, what would your options be?

—Well, we could move, if that was a possibility, or we could just not have the kid go to school, or there's a couple of other schools around, but that's about it for options.

—So what will the parents of my friends do?

—It's up to them.

A car crossed the overpass above us and Shelly opened her eyes and followed the sound like she'd followed the sound of the watchman's whistle that morning. The car passed behind her head until its sound faded away and then she closed her eyes but kept her head tilted back against the concrete, her chin tilted up, listening to the last sounds of the car disappearing. When there was no more sound, she let her chin and head fall forward so she was facing me.

—So Kendra? What will her parents do?

I put my head back against the concrete incline as Shelly had done.

—They'll probably move.

—Where?

—Wherever they're allowed to. I don't know.

—And Jessie?

—One of those new schools.

—The ones that cost?

—Yeah. Those.

—And me?

—We'll stay.

—But no school.

Shelly kept her eyes closed. The backs of her legs were flat against the concrete floor and the undersides of her arms lay flat against the concrete incline.

—No school, I said.

—Not even those other ones?

—Can't, I said.

She brought her arm up and opened her eyes and grasped her band. She tried to spin it around her wrist.

—It's so tight, she said.

—We'll get it adjusted.

—So who will teach me?

—I will, I said.

She tapped her finger on her kneecap, like she was counting something.

—Lucky I like biology.

—Yep.

She hugged her knees to her chest and laid her head on top of them, looking my way.

—We should study plants this year, she said.

—All year? I said.

—All year, she confirmed.

—Done, I said.

—And flowers, like those ones in your books.

—Flowering plants. All year. We can do that.

A semitrailer rattled over the joints that separated the bridge from the mainland asphalt. The tires snapped above us. The trailer's bulk flashed through a bar of light that lay diagonally across the opposite incline.

—You feeling better? I asked her.

She shrugged.

—That good, huh? I said.

She gave me a small smile and closed her eyes.

I put the back of my hand on her forehead and left it there.

—You're warm.

She shrugged her shoulders again.

—Did Grandpa say to do anything? I asked. She shook her head underneath my hand and I took it away. She opened her eyes.

—I don't think he has any medicine left, she said, looking at me over her forearms crossed on top of her knees. She coughed and the coughing almost unfolded all her small folded body parts but she gripped her arms around her little knees and held her creased body together against the rattles vibrating from her chest. I pulled her red ball cap off and pulled her black hair away from her face and put it behind her ear and back over her shoulder. She smiled softly again and sighed. I put the ball cap back on, backwards.

—Look, she said, her eyes focusing behind me, downstream.

A person on a bicycle came toward us, keeping out of the thin sheet of river water. When there was no way around the water, the rider stopped pedaling and lifted their feet from the pedals and coasted through the ribbon of water. Small plumes sprayed from both sides of the tires, then the feet came back down to the pedals. The rider had long black hair.

—Is that Jen? my niece asked.

I nodded.

Jen didn't pedal quickly. She wasn't in a hurry.

—What time is it? I asked.

My niece brought her head up from her forearms and turned to her backpack and unzipped the top zipper and ran her hand through the bag. Her hand moved through the adventure gear, grasping at the contents, and took out a wristwatch with no wristband. She turned it right side up.

—One o'clock, she said.

—Thanks, I said.

My ex slowly passed the painted names she had created and rode toward us up the aqueduct.

—When's the last time you were down here? my niece asked me. Her eyes were on Jen.

—Down where?

—Down here. To the river.

—I thought I told you that.

—You just said it was a long time ago. When it was a real river.

—Well, that sounds about right. When it was a real river.

I watched Jen come up the aqueduct. She was wearing a long dress, like my niece, dark though, with no ruffles or frills, just solid. She had it pushed up to her knees and her knees were drawn in together so she could pedal the bike.

—Hey, Shelly said.

—What?

She'd been talking to me.

—And the walls weren't here? she asked.

—No. Just the river.

—Just the water.

—Yeah. I told you this. And rocks. And more cottonwoods.

—Like that dead tree by the truck?

—Yeah. Like that one, I said. But with leaves. Green.

—What did you do? she asked.

—In the river?

—Yeah.

—I swam, I said.

—Swam? In this?

—I told you it wasn't like this.

—Who were you with?

Jen had a backpack on. She was close now. Her black hair was bleached slightly from the summer sun. The lightest parts of her hair were still dark, but dark like soil, not black next to black, but black next to any other color.

—I was with Jen, I said.

—I knew it, Shelly said.

—Whatever. You did not know it.

—I did, she said. I glanced at her and she was smiling. I turned back toward Jen. Shelly and I watched her coast the last few yards and cross into the shadow of the overpass.

—Your mom tells you too much, I whispered to Shelly, keeping my eyes on Jen. Shelly nudged me with her elbow.

Jen leaned her bike over and dismounted and the hem of her dress fell and covered the tennis shoes she wore. She threaded her thumbs under the straps of the backpack. I heard my niece take her first full and deep breath of the day. I took one too. A cliff swallow swung up to a row of abandoned nests underneath the bridge and shouted something loudly. It pecked at the empty mud nests, and bits of grass and dirt fell toward the floor. It watched the refuse fall to the concrete floor and flew away. Jen watched it pass out the other side of the underpass, out into the sunlight.

I couldn't see her face. Or I couldn't see it as well as I wanted to. She was backlit and my eyes couldn't make out her features through the contrast. Long strands of her almost-black hair fell around her ears and lay across her cheeks. There must have been a slight breeze where she stood, just a couple of yards away, because these strands of hair swung slightly, their ends rolling side to side across her chest. I could feel no breeze though. Her hair just swayed like this. Maybe it was cool air falling from the overpass's shadow and passing around her neck and shoulders. Or maybe she swayed slowly back and forth. I took another deep breath.

Jen put her hands on her hips. I still couldn't see her face well enough.

—You guys should leave, Jen said. They weren't the exact words I had wanted to hear come from her mouth.

—I know, I said.

—Hi, my niece said.

—Hey, baby, my ex said, her voice becoming soft and warm.

—We found a body, I said.

—You found a skeleton, she corrected me.

—How do you know that? I asked.

—There was a skeleton in the cooler in the back of your truck, she said. She put her hands back on the straps of her backpack. She rolled her feet out onto her ankles. Or that's what it looked like she was doing. Her dress covered her feet.

—I have her skull with me in my bag, Shelly said.

—What? I said.

My niece started to unzip her backpack and reach in. I put my arm on top of the pack. Shelly stopped and looked up.

—It's all right, baby, Jen said. You can leave it in there.

—Leave it in there, I said.

—We're trying to find out who she is, my niece said.

Jen stood quietly, looking at me or looking at Shelly, or still looking over to where that swallow had flown. I couldn't tell.

—Have you had them scan her band? Jen asked.

—No band, Shelly said. Her hand was cut off. You have any idea who she might be?

—This sounds more like a deal between a family and one of the sides, Jen said.

—Right, I said.

—Then why would I have any idea about who she is?

—I don't know. You hear things.

—The names I paint are from the wars. I don't receive names from anywhere else.

—Right.

—I get the lists and I come down here and paint. I don't hear anything.

—Okay, I said. Jen was mad now, maybe just frustrated, but she didn't want to hear any more about what I thought she might know.

My niece got to her feet.

—Where you going? I asked her.

—Into the sun. I'm cold. She walked away from us and crossed to the sunlight into which the swallow had flown. Shelly ran her hands up and down her arms and coughed loudly and she looked like she was going to bend over and start hacking like she had before but then she just kept walking, her yellow dress bright again in the sun. She stopped and sat with her back against the incline and her shoulders relaxed from the rigid position they had been in. Her eyes closed and she gently put her head against the red name painted there. She lifted her head slightly and put her cap on facing forward, pulling shade over her eyes.

—What's wrong with Shelly? Jen asked.

—We don't know, I said.

—You don't know?

—My dad thinks maybe it's just a cold.

—Sounds like pneumonia.

—It's not pneumonia, I said.

—How do you know that? I can hear her breathing from here.

—You don't cough up blood when you have pneumonia.

—She's coughing up blood?

I was glad I couldn't see Jen's face now.

I nodded.

—Then it's not just a cold.

I shook my head.

—Your dad knows about the blood?

—The blood just started again yesterday. It comes and goes.

—But he knows it's not just a cold.

—Probably.

—So you drag her out here on a fact-finding mission?

I didn't say anything.

—She should be home.

—My sister had to work. My mom and dad don't really do all-day daycare anymore.

Jen had a scar across her face from years before. I strained my eyes, trying to get a glimpse of it through the shadows.

—So what are you going to do for her then? she said.

She'd gotten the scar while we were running through a fence that surrounded someone's oilfield. I'd let the barbed wire up too soon. A rusty barb had caught her cheek.

—I don't know what we're going to do for her, I said.

The scar went from the corner of her eye to that taut skin just before the earlobe, where the jaw hinges and bulges. There had been blood immediately, but we'd been running, she hadn't felt it yet, and I hadn't told her about it. Safely away from the oiler and his shotgun, Jen put her hand up to wipe away what she must have thought was sweat. Looking at the blood on her hand, watching it run down her wrist, she didn't let out a sound. We kept moving, running, putting more space between us and the oiler, between us and that shotgun.

—She's yellow, right? Jen said, nodding toward Shelly.

—Yeah.

My niece lay there against the incline getting too much sun. Her chest ratcheted up in small gasps and then slowly fell down. Her eyes closed, her mouth opened, her head tilted back. The sun soaked into her black hair and into her yellow dress and she palmed the hot concrete like she had palmed the cool concrete in the shadows. Behind her the painted names converged at a point in the distance.

—I don't know what we're going to do for her, I said again.

Jen pushed her hair away from her face. She and my niece shared a hair color, along with their band color. She passed her finger over her scar. Which was her habit. Like she was trying to brush it away along with the loose strands of hair.

—You need a blue. Get her across, she said.

—We don't have money for that.

—Most people don't use money.

—We can't do that, I said.

—They did that to my brother.

I nodded my head slowly, acknowledging what she had said, surprised she had mentioned it.

—I remember, I said.

—You should, she said.

Shelly's head had fallen slightly to her side. It looked like she was asleep. Her chest wasn't moving much, just small, shallow breaths. She would wake up soon with a start, once her body couldn't deal with so little oxygen, like an old man sleeping too long on his back.

—When was the last time we saw each other? I asked, keeping my eyes on Shelly and away from Jen.

—I stay away from town, Jen said softly, gently, perhaps trying to apologize.

—Yeah. Me too.

—Not much chance of us seeing each other, she said.

—But when was the last time? I asked.

I watched her take her backpack off and put it on the ground beside her bike.

—Do they bother you guys anymore? she said.

—Which side?

—Either of them.

—No. Not directly.

—Not directly? she said.

—We can't get any medicine.

Shelly coughed and woke up gasping and we both looked out into the sun on the far side of the bridge and waited for Shelly to calm herself and get her breathing under control.

—But they're not trying to kill any of you, she said.

—Not quickly, I said. Shelly wiped some phlegm from her chin.

—That's good.

—That was the deal.

—Yeah. Her voice was quiet. She talked without moving. Except for those breezes through her hair, and her ankles, which she kept rolling.

—So nobody since her dad? Jen said.

I shook my head.

—How old is she? Jen asked.

—Ten in September.

She moved slightly now, unclasping her hands behind her back and letting her arms swing to her sides.

—There's something going on right now, she said. Some kind of change.

—That's what my dad said. My sister got stopped heading east of Conrad.

—Yeah. I heard about that one.

—You know what's going on? I asked her.

—No. Not yet.

—Names keep coming in like normal?

—Yeah, she said. But the points of revision. And the patrols. There's more of everything right now. Somebody is going to make a move. You're not going to be safe. Some of the oilfields will be back in play.

—I can get back south if I go east first, I said.

—Not too far east, she said, which was true. Too far east and we'd run into other factions. You need to forget about the cooler of bones.

I nodded, but not the kind of nodding that is meant to agree with what was just said.

—You're going to drag your sick niece all along the Front until you find the name of this dead girl? She was still talking quietly, but she was done apologizing, the gentleness in her voice gone. She grabbed the handle of her bike and lifted it and then bent and picked up her backpack.

—Why are you so interested in this girl? she asked, turning her bike around.

—I don't know. I just am.

—Well, that makes one of you, she said. She swung her backpack on. I could hear her spray-paint bottles rattling against one another.

—I have to get to work, she said.

—Yeah.

—You want me to give Shelly a ride?

I looked over. Shelly looked asleep. I couldn't see her eyes underneath the shadow of her ball cap.

—We'll walk, I said.

—Be careful, she said. There's something not right today. She pulled her dress up to her thighs and swung a foot over the seat of her bike and straddled it, still standing. Her hand dropped the dress and its middle rested on the top bar and the rest fell to her shins. Her shoulders went up and down, adjusting her backpack. She sat on the seat and her feet reached the pedals and she turned the bike around and moved out into the sun, away from the shadow of the bridge.

—Yell if you want me to come back and get her, she said, and rode down the concrete riverbed back to her paintings.

8
—Hey.

I felt a nudge on my shoulder.

—Hey, Shelly said again.

I opened my eyes. I'd fallen asleep. Shelly was standing next to me, gently putting her knee into my shoulder.

—Hey, I said.

—Where did Jen go?

I looked down the aqueduct and couldn't quite bring anything into focus. I waited. My eyes closed again, trying to flush the blurs out of them.

—Hey, Shelly said again.

—Wait. I opened my eyes and looked again down the river, clearer now. There she is, I said. My head tilted toward her. My niece followed where my head had pointed. We could hear Jen shaking one of her paint cans, dim and hollow.

—You see her? I said, following the sound first, then focusing in on the black dot that represented her.

—No, Shelly said. Well, kind of.

—Where are your glasses? I asked her.

—In my backpack. She didn't move to put them on, just kept squinting down the aqueduct.

The small dot of Jen walked up the opposite incline and then turned and ran down it, gaining some momentum to carry her across the flat riverbed and up the incline to where she was working. Her legs weren't visible, hidden by her long dark dress. She floated up the incline with no noticeable foot movements and then she crouched down into an even smaller dot. The spray sound of the paint didn't make it to us. Silence, then a hollow rattle, then silence. Then she floated back down to the concrete riverbed and went to her backpack for a new color. Shelly coughed.

—You ready? I asked my niece.

—Yeah, she said.

I took her hand and she stepped back and let her body fall away from me to help me to my feet. We walked into the sun. I walked with my eyes closed, the light too much for my eyes to take.

—How long did we nap for? I asked her. We walked holding hands. I hoped she was looking where we were going.

—How long did you nap for, she corrected.

—You didn't nap? I asked. I peeked at her. I could only see one of her eyes under the brim of her cap. It was closed.

—No.

—You were awake the whole time? I said. I closed my eyes.

—Yeah.

—Hmm, I said.

Shelly's palm was sweaty and cold, her breaths truncated before they could fully inflate her lungs.

—Try to take some slow bigger breaths, I said.

—I'm trying.

—Okay.

She pressed her fingers around mine in pulses, clenching tightly each time her breath ran through another barbed section in her lungs. I could feel her trying to work through all these nettles, trying to do what I had said, get that full breath, make me feel as though she was okay.

—Are you watching where we are going? I asked.

—No, she said, pausing from her breathing to answer me.

—Neither am I, I said.

She exhaled and I peeked again and she smiled faintly and tried for another deeper breath.

—Just relax, I said. I dropped her cold hand and pulled her next to me as we kept walking.

—It's hot, she said.

—If I let you go then both of us are going to have to open our eyes, I said.

—Okay.

I let my arm fall from around her shoulders and we both opened our eyes and began trying to adjust to the light reflecting at us from both inclines. She put a hand on each side of her cap.

—Nice technique, I said. That work?

—Pretty good, she said.

We came to the first ribbon of river to cross and Shelly didn't drop her hands from her cap to lift her dress. She walked straight through the flat river and turned around and looked briefly at our tracks on the dry river floor and then spun back around. She dropped one of her hands from her cap and gripped mine, with a surge of pressure, and then regripped my fingers and settled her fingers in with mine again.

We came to where Jen was painting and we stopped and watched.

—Can you throw me the blue? Jen said.

I let go of Shelly's hand and walked to the backpack and ran my hand through the cans.

—Light blue, she said.

I found it and walked to where the incline met the flat and she pivoted on her heels and held her hand out. I lobbed the can to her. She lobbed the can she was finished with and the cans crossed in the air. She corralled hers between her forearm and her chest and I moved to catch the one she'd thrown to me. I put it in with the others.

—You're a good drawer, my niece said.

I nudged her with my elbow.

—Thanks, baby, Jen said. She stopped working and turned toward us.

—It's pretty. Your painting, Shelly said.

—How you feeling, baby? Jen asked.

—Okay, Shelly said.

—I like your dress, Jen said to her. Shelly twisted happily back and forth and the lacy yellow hem of her dress fluttered in the white sunlight that was landing all around us. She pressed herself into my thigh, like she was shy.

—I like yours, Shelly said. Jen smiled.

—Why don't you head up to the truck? I said to Shelly. I handed her the keys.

—Okay, she said.

—You know which key it is?

She nodded and turned and started walking. The ends of her shoe-laces slapped front and back around her ankles and the loose rubber soles slapped against her toes. She hopped a step, and then skipped two, walked a few more steps, then skipped twice more, then returned to walking.

—So you don't know anything about the skeleton? Jen asked. We both kept our eyes on Shelly.

—No. She's probably thirteen. Fourteen, I said.

Shelly kicked a rock, like we had on the way to the bridge. She stopped to watch it bounce over the concrete and skip over the sliver of river. I couldn't see where the rock stopped. She kept walking.

My ex's dark hair covered her face where her scar was. She had put a cap on to help with the sun. Her face was in a shadow like it had been under the bridge. She turned toward me for a moment and her hair swung away and the scar appeared briefly and then was covered again. She might have been looking at me. I still couldn't tell.

—Go to Phillip's house, she said.

Shelly started climbing diagonally up the incline to the truck, bend-ing over and holding herself steady with one hand to the concrete. She got to the top and stepped back and looked over the steep decline of the aqueduct.

—Get in the truck, baby, I yelled to her. My voice seemed to dis-appear before it even left my mouth. I wondered if she had heard me.

Shelly stepped away from the edge and I couldn't see her anymore. I didn't like not being able to see her.

—She's sick, Jen said.

—I know. I'll figure something out.

—You have water?

I shook my head. Not much, I said. We were both looking to see if Shelly would come back in sight.

—You need to get some, she said. I nodded.

—Why Phillip's house? I asked. He was one of the ones who took your brother.

—I know.

—So why him? What does he know? I asked.

—He's trying to get out. It's never worked for him.

Phillip had always been swept up with those he found himself surrounded by, never able to make his own way. I remembered him as having a good heart, as someone who wanted to be good, but he just hadn't been able to push back enough when people had other ideas for his good heart. My sister and I had never been friends with him. Jen's family had tried to take him in various times, but it had never stuck. The forces of other people had been overpowering. I wished we had stepped in harder for him. Maybe that would have made the difference. Maybe if my family and Jen's family had joined forces, our combined pull would have been enough. He didn't have a family of his own to ever go back to, so he'd drift for a bit, he'd steal from neighbors to survive, then the opportunity to join a side came up and that's what he did. It hadn't worked out for him, but it had worked out for his side. I couldn't picture how Phillip would get out, and I couldn't see how he'd be able to help us now.

—What's Phillip going to tell us? I asked.

—If his side knows anything about disappeared people down by the reservoir, he could find out.

—By asking people on his side?

Jen nodded. I shrugged my shoulders.

—You don't have much going for you, she said. Nobody's going to care about some bones found down at the reservoir.

I looked back down toward the bridge of the highway and past that, to where the scribble of water and all the names on either side met at one point, a point that my eyes couldn't seem to focus on. I wasn't sure why I had put the bones in the cooler; I wasn't sure why Shelly's argument for finding the identification of the dead girl had convinced me to try to do so. People had stopped looking for the disappeared years ago. We had certainly come across other bones and we'd had no problem leaving them where they were. Our society had evolved beyond the point where we'd once cared about these people. They had become the norm. To disappear was expected. For anyone to reappear—alive or otherwise—was unexpected. Shelly had somehow convinced me to take the unexpected route, like we might have done years before. Being with her was like living twenty years ago. She still thought like we thought back then.

—Hand me the other blue, Jen said. She tossed me the can of light blue she'd made a few strokes with and I caught it. I dropped it in the backpack and found the darker blue and lobbed it up to her.

—So what's not right? What's different today? I said. Why the increase in points of revision? Why are there extra patrols out?

—I don't know, she said.

—The contracts don't matter anymore? I said.

—Something like that. I don't know. Feels like everything's in play again. She sprayed another layer onto the name she was crouching over, mixing the blues. You should go.

—Yeah, I said. We should go. I turned to start walking down the aqueduct, anxious to get to my niece. The tiny pebbles scratched beneath my shoes softly and hollowly as I pivoted. I wanted to say something else. Maybe just goodbye. I just started walking instead.

—Her fourth birthday, I heard Jen say.

—What? I said, turning around.

—When we last saw each other.

I thought for a bit. It could have been. Seemed too long though.

—Then her dad was taken, Jen added. Which was right. Jen was right.

—A long time, I said.

—Yeah. And then all the rest happened.

—Yeah, I said.

She started to say more but stopped. She was always confident, always sure of herself. Moments of indecision for her, like this moment now, did not come frequently. She tried to say something again. I watched her, interested in what she might say, if she'd try to clarify other things that had happened back when we'd last seen each other, back when her brother had died and all the rest had happened.

—Take care of her, she said, and kept trying to say something more.

—I'd do anything for her. I watched and waited again.

—You might have to, she said, and then her self-assuredness came back, any doubt or confusion washing itself away, and she didn't quite shrug her shoulders, she didn't quite motion that she was giving up on the idea of saying anything after that, but she simply returned her attention to the name in front of her and readied the spray can.

My hand rose to wave goodbye but it didn't make it past my waist. It didn't want to wave goodbye to her, for one reason or another. I let it fall to my side.

9 —Why aren't you in the truck? I asked.

—Too hot, Shelly said. She handed the keys back to me.

She leaned against the guardrail and found a spot where the dead cottonwood's shadow covered her head and the rest of her body, and then she leaned her chest back over the rail and into the sun, toward the aqueduct, to watch Jen on the flat concrete, searching through her backpack for a new color. Jen grabbed a can of the color she needed and drifted, in her long dress, to the far side of the concrete river as she had before. She scaled the opposite incline a few yards, and then descended and floated across the aqueduct and rose up to the name she was working on, a little higher than where she'd been. She folded to all fours, leaning against the slanted concrete, and again the sound of the spray can shaking filled the void of the barren river. I leaned farther over the guardrail to better see her working. Shelly leaned farther, too. I leaned a little more to see past Shelly.

—She's beautiful, my niece said.

—Yeah, I said.

Shelly turned from the guardrail and faced the truck again, pushing herself up onto the guardrail to sit. Her red shoes swung up off the ground and she rubbed them together. All the red reservoir dust was gone and nothing more rubbed off of them.

—There're two of us, she said, still focusing on her shoes, still rubbing them together.

—Two of us what? I said.

—Two of us interested in the girl. Not just you. Not just one.

She clapped her shoes together twice and then was done with them, leaving them hanging, unmoving, in the air beneath her, and turned her head up to me.

—You hear too much, I said.

—I hear just enough.

—Too much.

—Just enough.

I leaned back against the railing. I was in the sun. The thin upper branches of the dead cottonwood didn't offer any shade against the hot white light that came through them.

—That's good, I said. It's good to have two.

—Twice as good, she said.

—And sometimes even more.

—Yep, she said, and she pushed herself off the guardrail and went to her backpack, which was leaned up against the front wheel of the truck. In the backpack she found the distributor cap and handed it to me.

—Thanks, I said. Shelly had convinced me, I think, about the bones. And if I was still hesitant about my new interest in the bones, that hesitance was dissipating. I didn't quite know why, though. Maybe my interest was just surpassing my hesitation, but the hesitation was still there. If my interest waned, my hesitation might come back. That would mean it had never left, it had just been covered for a while until something came along and uncovered it, or until something came along to push me into a more realistic point of view.

—Who's Phillip and where's his house? she said.

—How much did you hear down there?

—Just enough, she said.

—Why'd you leave the doors of the truck open?

I popped the hood and worked on the battery and the distributor.

—It was hot in there, she said.

—Letting it air out, I said.

—Yeah.

—Good thinking.

I brought the hood down and let it close. I pushed on it to make sure it was shut.

We climbed into the cab but the seats were still too hot and we both jumped out.

—So hot, she said.

—Check under the seat over there.

She bent her head in front of the seat and stuck her hand underneath and pulled out a jacket and a pair of pants.

—You need to clean your truck, she said.

—Heat shields, I said.

Shelly threw me the jacket and kept the pants and we folded them and put them on our seats. We got back in.

—Better? I asked.

She fine-tuned her heat shield placement, wiggling herself and moving the pants at the same time, then came to a rest.

—Yes. She went to grab her seatbelt and then remembered it didn't work.

—What grade were you supposed to be going into this year?

—Fourth. I'm short for my age.

—Not too short.

—Thanks.

She sat up straight and looked satisfied with what she could see over the dashboard.

—To Phillip's house? I said.

Strands of her hair fell over her eyes and she took her cap off and hooked it over one of her knees while she pulled her hair behind her head and held it there. As she put her hat back on, she pulled a big clump of hair through the opening in the back and patted the cap into place with both hands.

—To Phillip's house, she said.

—So much hair, I said.

—I love it, she said. Just like my mom's.

I started the truck and Shelly rolled down her window.

—My seat is still kind of hot, she said.

—Mine too.

—What do we tell my mom if she calls?

—You tell her whatever you want, I said.

—I'll just tell her the truth.

—That sounds perfect.

We headed west toward the refuse dumps, mounds of mine tailings stretched out thin and flat and red. Shelly pushed her hands down over her thighs like she had before, flattening her dress. She held her hands tightly over her knees and the wrinkles disappeared from the shiny yellow fabric, then she released her hands and the wrinkles popped back. She put her hands flat on her hips and ran them down to her knees once more. She pressed her dress tightly to her thighs and brought her feet up and there were her red shoes.

—You okay? I asked her.

—I'm okay, she said.

We crested a small hill and came out onto another field of oil pumps, black bulges of iron sitting atop the brown landscape, and as we entered the field the wind brought the whining sound of their wheel houses into the cab. Between the oil pumps there were people walking. Not many. Two or three over to the right, and then three or four more to the left. They wandered. And a few others were in the shadows cast by the oil pumps. They rested, sheltered from the sun. These people were hard to see. The darkness of the iron and the blackness of the shadows and the burnt and bronzed skin of those who sat in this blackness did not easily distinguish themselves from one another. The lack of light blended one with the other. These small groups of people walked right past each other, those going east passing those headed west, those going south passed ones headed north.

—Where are they going? Shelly asked.

—I'm not sure, I said.

—What are they looking for?

The small groups, or families, fragments of families, didn't acknowledge the other fragments. There was no common thread that unified them. They all searched for shelter, for protection, but they'd never find it. And they knew they'd never find it. Nobody wanted them.

—Are we like them? Shelly asked.

—Not yet, I said. A line of water trucks passed us heading east and I gripped the steering wheel against the gusts of wind each brought toward us.

—Water, Shelly said.

—Yep.

—No. Water, Shelly said again after the trucks had passed.

—What?

She pointed at a run-down building on the road to the right. It was a bar. A guard stood leaning against a mangled billboard that stood in the gravel lot outside the bar's front door.

—Oh. Good idea, I said.

I braked hard and put my hand across Shelly's shoulder, to keep her in her seat, and I pulled over to the side of the road. I backed up while a car passed on the left, he beeped and yelled something at us as he went by, and then we were in the bar's parking lot. I backed the truck past the watchman leaning against a post of the old billboard and pulled next to the only other car in the lot.

—I don't want to wait here, Shelly said.

—I know. You won't. You're coming in.

—Okay, she said.

—Leave your backpack. Bring a couple plastic bottles.

She reached behind the seat and found three bottles. She handed me one and slid off the seat onto the ground and turned around and swung her door shut. We met at the back of the truck and walked up to the door of the bar. The door's window was blacked out. I pulled it open and Shelly walked through. I looked back at the watchman and we nodded at each other and then I went into the bar and let the door close behind me and stood for a moment letting my eyes adjust to the darkness. I couldn't see Shelly and then she tapped me on the arm. She was right beside me.

—We're not open yet.

Someone behind the bar was talking to us. There was another someone at the bar hunched over.

—We just need some water, I said.

—We're not open yet.

—Just some water.

—She's not allowed in here.

—She needs to use the bathroom.

Shelly looked up at me.

—Give me your bottles. Go to the bathroom, I said.

—Where? she said.

—Back there.

I pointed to a light in the back of the room.

—I don't . . . , she started.

—Just go. Or wait in the truck, I said.

The neon lights of the beer signs started to illuminate the room and I saw the man who'd been talking. I walked to the bar and watched Shelly head back to the bathroom.

—We don't have any water, the man said.

He walked into the light of the television that hung above the bar. I put the plastic bottles up on the bar.

—No water, he said.

—Just one bottle, I said.

The man's face reflected the colors flashing on the television. The man who was hunched over at the bar stirred awake and lifted his head. He focused on the bartender and then turned his head toward me and then toward Shelly as she came by my side and pushed her shoulder into my hip.

—It was locked, she said.

—Okay.

The man down the bar mumbled something and spun his stool toward us. He focused on Shelly. I pushed a plastic bottle toward the bartender. The drunk pushed his hand down the bar toward us, steadying himself as he went, his feet nearing the floor as he slid off his stool. I took a few bills from my shirt pocket, still watching the drunk, his mumbling quieter now, but closer, and I put two of the bills on the bar and pushed them to the bartender. His hand swept them up and he turned and held them to the light of the television to read their worth. He put them in his shirt pocket and took the smallest of our bottles, one of the two I hadn't slid toward him. He walked away.

—This one, I said to him, holding up a bigger bottle, but he just shook his head and didn't turn around. I couldn't see what else he was selling. The bar didn't have any refrigerators, no taps. The drunk was on his feet now, but I couldn't tell what he was drunk on. He had no glass or can in front of him. He put one hand on the bar and slid it steadily closer to us through the dim light. A ring on his wedding finger ran along the smooth edge of the bar. Two stools away now, he pushed himself forward. His thighs cleared a path through the stools as he neared us.

His free hand reached for Shelly and I pushed my hand into his throat and, lifting him free of the bar, I walked him back toward to his stool. His wedding ring slipped off the waxy surface of the bar and his feet started to support him. My thumb was pressed into the back of one side of his jaw and the rest of my fingers were pressed into the other, squeezing his face. The man gasped a bit. I lifted him more until he let go of the bar with his one steadying hand and was standing by himself, both hands pulling at my forearm, trying to loosen my hand from his throat, and I set him back down on his stool. I let go and he took a big breath in and turned toward the bar and gasped some more and hunched back over and sat quietly, laboring air through his lungs.

The bartender came back and looked at the man and slid the bottle back over the bar to me. I grabbed the two empty bottles and gave them to Shelly. The drunk man was slouched over as he had been when we entered.

—Let's go, I said to Shelly.

We walked out and stood still trying to readjust to the afternoon light, the whiteness of it, the dusty haze catching all the burning sunlight. Shelly had her eyes closed, her hands at her sides, each one grasping a plastic bottle. The left one gripped its bottle and released, then the right one gripped and released, the hard crinkling sounds of the empty plastic filling the bright light that fell around us.

—Stop that, I said.

Her hands stopped pulsing around their bottles. I peeked down at her and her eyes were already wide open and looking across the parking lot. I squinted against the whiteness of the gravel and saw the man still leaning against the post of the tattered billboard. Shelly focused on him. My eyes couldn't take the light anymore and I looked back down at my feet.

—You ready? Shelly said.

—Wait a minute, I said.

I wiped away tears from the corners of my eyes and pushed them down over my cheeks.

—You okay? Shelly asked me.

—I'm fine, I said.

—Okay, she said.

—Let's go.

10 We left the parking lot of the bar and were back on the road. The mine tailings came back into view as we came out of a draw. The skull had been riding between Shelly and me and she picked it up and set it on her lap. There wasn't much more dust left to be smudged off by her thumbs but they went to work on it again.

—That man in the bar . . . , Shelly started, her face staying focused on her thumbs and the dull white of the girl's forehead.

—Which one? I said.

—The one, she said.

I didn't want to talk about it. I didn't say anything. Shelly looked up from the skull to gauge my face, to assess my mood, and then went back to concentrating on its forehead.

—The one, she said again, the one that wanted to hurt me.

I tapped the steering wheel quietly, pinky to pointer, thinking. I exhaled heavily.

—What? she said.

Her thumbs went harder at the forehead then moved to the concave area of the temple to find dust that she'd missed.

—Nothing. I'm sorry.

And I was sorry. More for me, for a moment, and then I got myself together and was sorrier for her. Sorry she didn't have an uncle who could explain any of this to her.

—He didn't want to hurt you, I said

She looked at me.

—He did, she said.

Which was right. He would have hurt her.

—He didn't know what he wanted, I tried.

—He wanted to hurt me though, she said. He was moving at me. Then you stopped him. You stopped him because you knew what he wanted to do.

—Yeah, I agreed.

She looked up from the skull again, gauging something else on my face. She didn't say anything for the moment. Shelly was an expert at waiting for a reply if she thought that was the best option, or if she thought the silence made things a bit more difficult for me than for her. I moved my hands to the bottom of the steering wheel and started to say something but stopped. My hands tilted outward toward my wrists, stretching themselves, and my shoulders shrugged inward for a moment but no words came out. The heat and the light and the smell of the flares we passed were all immense. She waited some more.

—He didn't know what he wanted to do, I said. His brain's gone. It's not there anymore. All that shit he pumped into his body eroded it away. There's just a couple neurons up there now, and now and then they send an impulse to his body and something happens. Maybe he just wanted to hug you. Maybe you reminded him of his daughter. I don't know.

—But you weren't going to take a chance, she said, and she looked up and I didn't know how much of all I'd said she'd understood but she seemed to understand that I hadn't liked doing what I'd done but that I'd done it and I was still trying to work it out in my own mind.

—That's right, I said. I wasn't going to take a chance.

She tipped the skull right side up and rested her elbow on it again.

—Thank you, she said.

—I didn't want to do what I did, I said.

—Kind of like him? she said.

I thought for a minute and didn't think she was right, but she was right. I'd just reacted. There hadn't been any more thought than that put into it. I'd grabbed his throat and lifted his waiflike body up. I couldn't argue any differently.

—Kind of like him, I said.

—That's okay, she said. Thank you.

—Of course, I said.

It was silent for a bit more but it was comfortable. Shelly seemed okay with how I'd tried to explain things.

—Why do you think she was in the reservoir like that? she asked.

—In the reservoir dead?

—No, she said.

She brought strands of hair that were loose in the wind back behind her ears.

—I mean, why do you think she had a broken hand?

—A sawed-off hand, I said.

—A sawed-off hand, then.

She squeezed the skull between her knees so it wouldn't roll anywhere. Her right hand moved to her left wrist and she rotated her yellow band.

—Someone probably wanted her band, I said.

—Someone needed it more than she did, she said.

—That's not exactly right, I said.

—What is exactly right?

I took the truck across the rumble strips on the right to miss a pothole.

—Well, there's nothing exactly right, I said.

—How could that be?

—What be? I said.

—How could there not be anything exactly right? Her eyes looked at me through her hair that had fallen back across her face. She left it swaying there while she waited for my answer. She didn't wait long this time.

—Her family didn't need it as much as someone else's, she said.

—No. You can't say that, I said.

—I just said it.

—I mean, just wait a minute.

—But it's pretty close to that, she said.

—Her family just couldn't protect her enough probably, I said.

—How could that be possible?

—The other family, or other people, just did more to get it.

—Did more? she asked.

—Right.

She put her hands back on the skull and turned it to face her.

—Her family couldn't protect her, she said.

—That's right.

—But not exactly right, she said.

—That's right.

—They wanted to, but just couldn't. She put the skull back on the seat between us and pressed her hands to her dress to take the wrinkles away.

—Do you remember when they took your dad away? I asked her.

—Of course, she said. Her hands let the wrinkles come back and then they pulled them tight again and held them away.

—You were young.

—I was four, she said.

I thought about the four-year-old she had been and whether she could have remembered anything about what had happened. I tried to remember what kind of kid I was at four years old and whether I could have remembered anything or understood anything.

—What are you thinking about? Shelly said.

—About when I was four.

—What about it?

—Whether I remember anything about it.

—Do you?

We got to a gravel road and I took it north toward a hill that sat in the near distance.

—No, I don't think so, I said.

—Nothing? Try harder.

—It's just blank, Shelly.

—Like how blank? How can that be?

—I don't know.

—I remember them coming for my dad, she said. I remember their truck.

—What did the truck look like? We had spoken about this day only a handful of times, always when we thought Shelly wasn't around or when she was asleep in the car or off a little ways, playing. If she had picked up memories from our conversations, they could have only been general. A truck and nothing more. She was four. I had no memories of four.

—The truck was red, she said.

She had that correct. Perhaps we had spoken about a red truck.

—There were five men, she said. That wasn't quite right.

—Two were women, she said. The rest were men. That was right.

—How do you remember that? I said.

—How don't you remember anything? she said, her eyes looking up toward me, almost dismissively, and then she looked forward again. What's up this hill?

I took the truck to the crest of the hill and stopped. The gravel road turned into two ruts with a high center. The ruts continued down the far side of the hill for a hundred yards or more and ended in front of a small square house.

—He was blue, she said.

I didn't think she would remember her dad's band.

—Like you, she added. I nodded, keeping my gaze on the house so I wouldn't have to look at her just yet. What are we doing up here? she asked.

—That's Phillip's house, I said. I lifted my hand from the steering wheel to point out the only house visible to us. She stopped looking at me and looked at the house. We sat for a minute. The oiljacks scattered around the house were the only things that moved. A few flares sent smoke into the air. The house had one door in the front. This front door had a three-step walk-up but none of the steps were there. It was a common house on the Front, made even more common by the glass knocked out of its windows and its roof covered only in tattered tarpaper. There were no trees or bushes or signs of life outside the house. The paint was gone on its southern side, which meant the western side would be worn bare, almost to the studs, stripped away by the dust-filled winds that came from the mountains of mine tailings.

—You remember Phillip? I asked her. She shook her head.

—This is his house? she asked.

—Yeah.

Shelly's attention focused on the house.

—Who's Phillip? she said.

—He's one of the men. I snuck a peek at her and her eyebrows came together briefly and then relaxed again.

—Which one? she asked.

—What do you mean?

—That one with the glasses? There had been one with glasses.

—No, no glasses.

She reached again for her memory, her eyes squinting at the house, as if she were trying to see through its threadbare siding to catch a glimpse of Phillip, if he was inside.

—That one with the short hair? Shorter than yours?

—Yeah. Shorter than mine, I said. Shelly nodded and stopped squinting at the house. I let my foot fall off the brake and we coasted down the slight decline through the ruts. Dry weeds between the dusty tracks scraped against the underside of the truck. We rolled slowly to the house and I stopped a few yards from the porch that wasn't there. I opened my door and stepped out of the truck.

—Am I coming? Shelly asked.

—No.

She'd opened her door, having expected a yes, and I looked her back in to her seat. She shut her door.

—Just stay here. I slid out and swung the door shut. An upside-down bucket sat where the porch should have been.

—You think he's home? she said through the windshield. Her voice was muffled, dim. I told her to keep quiet. The screen door had long ago been ripped off. The front door was cracked open and I stood with my waist at the threshold and pushed it farther inward. It swung without sound and gently knocked against the wall. I stepped onto the bucket and then up onto the linoleum that covered the entrance to the house.

The living room was to the left and the kitchen to the right. A wall had separated the two but it was gone. The stove and fridge were missing. A couch with no cushions sat askew in the living room. A chair with a broken leg lay on its side. The subfloor showed through in places. Pools of dry dirt stained the linoleum where it was still intact. Footprints tracked through and beyond these dry puddles.

I took a step inside. A hallway led from the kitchen, a bathroom on the left and a bedroom on the right. I could see the couch cushions on the floor of the bedroom. A foot hung off the edge of one. I pushed the bedroom door like I had the front door and it swung the same way, brushing slightly over worn carpet. A body lay on the cushions face up. Its eyes were open, looking out its bedroom window. It was Phillip, pale and skinny and shirtless, his chest sunk in and his ribs bulging under his skin. He turned and looked at me and whispered something. He asked for water, mouthing the words without sounds, his tongue tapping on dark abysses where there should have been teeth. He started to move his right hand but it was chained to a stud that someone had dug through the drywall to get at, using it as an anchor. There were marks where he'd clawed at the stud, claw marks and blood. His eyes tried to focus on me but they sank back in their sockets. His skin strung itself tightly from his cheeks to his jawbones. His other hand was free and its fingernails were cracked and had been torn away from clawing at the two-by-four and at himself. A line of deep wounds led from his armpit to his belly button. His pants were stained brown and the couch cushion was stained, too. A needle, a plastic bottle with an inch of water left in it, and a dozen packets of magic were at the side of the bed, lying on the ratty carpet. They'd set up an apparatus so he could cook the water and the magic and shoot it all with one hand. A bungee cord lay coiled around itself on the couch cushion. The arm chained to the wall was bruised all along its veins. He had needle marks in his neck too.

—How long you been here chained up? I asked him.

His lips knocked off one another and his gums thumped together. I couldn't understand anything. Then he asked for water again. I could understand that.

—Water, he said, but there was no sound. He started nodding and then lost his train of thought and turned his head to the window, where it had been focused before, staring at some point far off. Drink the water or cook the magic with it. Those were the choices they'd left Phillip with.

I kicked the bottom of his bare foot and he snapped back to and glared at me, not out of anger, but out of fear. He tried to push himself up against the wall but his free hand slipped off the cushions each time he tried. I watched him struggle until he was still again. Neither of us moved. We just watched each other for a moment. He dug his heels in and gained some ground. He did another pass with his heels and gripped the chain that anchored him to the wall and managed a few more inches. His head slowly pushed higher on the pillow until it was against the wall, a few inches from the tornout drywall and the bare two-by-four. He stopped there, out of breath from such exertion.

—When did they chain you up? I asked him. I couldn't stop looking at him. The only thing that draws the eye more than a dead person is one dying. He had a gray band and it fit loosely around his chained-up wrist, falling almost to his elbow. If I'd had the bottle of water we'd bought at the bar I would have thrown it to him. He would have fumbled with it and struggled to unscrew the cap. But he would have gotten it open eventually and he would have gulped it all down in one tilt and then puked it all back up.

I walked over to the scattered sleeves of magic instead. Each sleeve was a wrapper of thin plastic the size of a sugar packet. I knelt down and poured a tablespoon of the water they had left him into the crucible and flicked on the lighter and began cooking him a double, something big enough to put him away. Phillip wasn't coming back from where he was headed. He gave a couple more kicks with his heels against the couch cushions, to sit up nice and straight and attentive, and forgot all about the water he'd been asking for. He used both hands to pull on the chain, then he pushed his free hand through his short blond hair, keeping it there, on top of his head, for a moment. His eyes opened wide and he looked from the small crucible to my face and back to the crucible, in quick little jerks of his head, and when the flame was going he just stared at that, waiting until the thin gray line of smoke started to come off the surface of the melting junk, boiling the half ounce of water. I opened a third packet and poured it on top of the other two, making sure none of the magic touched the bare skin of my fingers.

—Give me your arm, I said. He extended his untouched, unchained arm to me, soft side up, and I tied off the bungee cord above his bicep and his veins showed softly below the surface of his skin. The three packets had combined into one puddle and I cut the flame. I pulled the junk into his syringe and held it up between us. I asked him again how long he'd been tied up here. He just stared at the drops of magic coming from the needle.

—Here, I said, and he turned his clean forearm up to me again and he watched the needle pop the surface of his skin and find its vein. I pushed in the magic. His head thumped back softly against the wall. His toes curled and uncurled. I pulled out the needle and placed it with the remaining magic and left the room. The yellow flash of Shelly's dress turned from the bedroom doorway. When I came to the end of the hallway she was at the threshold of the front door, facing backwards, her foot searching for the up-side-down bucket. She found her footing and lowered the other one and then just stood on the bucket and looked at me.

—Hey, she said. She had her red ball cap on. Her hair mostly covered her face.

—Get in the truck, I said, softly, almost a whisper.

11 We pulled back on the road and headed west again, toward the tailing dumps. A wind had picked up and thin strips of red dust hovered over the asphalt and we drove through them, disrupting the patterns they made until they put themselves back together behind us.

—Sorry, Shelly said. I took my eyes from the rearview mirror, where I watched the red ribbons of sand remake themselves, and looked forward again.

—Okay, I said.

—Was that medicine? she asked.

—It wasn't medicine, I said.

—What was it? she said.

—Shelly, when I ask you to stay in the truck, I need you to stay in the truck, okay?

—Yeah, she said.

We descended into a draw and the wind disappeared and with it the red dust and its repeating waves of little lines. Shelly's head dropped. Her dress had two loose ends of a yellow ribbon that ran through little yellow hoops at her waist and she brought them together and tied them off and let her hands fall on her lap. She held her hands there, the fingers of one hand threaded with the fingers of the other.

—Was Phillip bad? she asked. Her head didn't rise. She put one thumb on top of the other.

—Phillip wasn't bad, I said.

—Even though he took away my dad?

—That's right.

—But you didn't like him?

I tried not to move, tried not to indicate one way or the other. I shook my head though, and she looked up, squinting at the glints of sun coming through the cracks in the windshield.

—Phillip was in an impossible spot, I said.

—So you didn't like the spot?

—I didn't like the spot.

—So what did you do to him?

—Nothing good, Shelly, I said.

She seemed like she wouldn't say anything more about it. She shouldn't have seen what I'd done, shouldn't have seen Phillip like that, shit coming from his pants, pus coming from his fried arms. Maybe she'd seen it all now. I couldn't think of anything she hadn't seen. Too much for a kid. But there weren't many kids on the Front who had seen less.

—You took him away from the spot, she said.

I nodded my head. I did, I said. Phillip's not in this spot anymore.

She nodded. I hoped she understood that his spot was not our spot, that there were different spots people were in and that some were okay. Although I wasn't sure if I believed that—that our spot was different than his. Maybe a little bit, maybe right now. Right now we were still okay. We might be all right. Helping Phillip was something we should have done a long time ago. Not doing so had brought his life to its recent end, and we had helped him on his way down this path.

—Look at that, Shelly said. She pointed to a kid on a bike, pedaling on the side of the road up ahead. We descended farther into the draw and the kid disappeared. I pushed on the gas but it didn't do much. We climbed out of the draw and the biker came back into view. The biker was a boy with a ball cap on. We pulled up beside him and I slowed down. He glanced at us and stopped pedaling for an instant and then turned forward and resumed his hurried pedaling. He took his bike to the outside of the rumble strips to make room for us to continue by. The red ribbons of dust were back. The boy had his head down, using the visor of his cap to shield his eyes.

The bike was too small for him, even though he was a small boy, no bigger than Shelly. His knees bounced up to his chest and back down, making it look like he was holding steady at some exaggerated speed, but he moved slowly along the highway, working hard to move himself at such a slow pace. His feet spun quickly around the crank. He bounced up and down off his seat. He couldn't pedal any faster. There was a headwind against him. And the dust.

He glanced at my niece, leaning on the ledge of her open window. We were on a decline now but he didn't stop pedaling. I let him pull in front of us a little so I could see him better. Another small incline started in a hundred yards. He had his cap pulled down tightly on his head. His stamina was impressive. He didn't stop pedaling. We caught back up to him. My niece leaned out the window again.

—Jake, she yelled.

—You know him? I asked.

She didn't say anything. Neither did Jake. He pedaled. Wisps of brown hair stuck out from under the sides of his cap. They bounced with each stroke he gave to the pedals.

—Where you going? Shelly asked. We were on the incline now. His pedaling slowed.

—You need a ride? she asked.

He just kept pedaling, not lifting his head. He doubled his efforts to fight the incline. He glanced up the road. The incline continued for a distance. The brim of his cap went back down and he kept pedaling.

—Is he a long ways from home? I asked my niece.

—You're a long ways from home, Shelly said to Jake. We were almost halfway up the incline now. The truck inched along.

—We have a skeleton, Shelly said to him.

The boy didn't flinch. It was unclear if he had even heard her. He just kept pumping his feet. Sweat shone on his face, where it ran down from his cap.

—Here's her skull, Shelly said, and lifted it out the window.

—Jesus, Shelly, put that down, I said.

Jake looked this time, stopped pedaling briefly, then put his head down even more, determined to outlast us.

Dust flew up into my eyes and I slowed the truck as I closed my eyes to clean them out.

—Don't do that, I said to Shelly.

—Do what?

—Moving that skull around and making it all dusty in here.

—There's not any more dust on it, she said.

I got my eyes open again as we crested the hill. I pushed the gas pedal back down to catch up with Jake. The dumps weren't where they should have been on the horizon anymore. Or maybe they were blocked from view by one more hill. Then Shelly and I saw a huge cloud of red hanging low on the horizon. It was where the red lines had come from. The red lines were gone now though. The red was in the air. Another jet of dust came through the cab, thicker now. The red on the horizon kicked itself into a cloud and rose high above us. Red streaks blew past us and bent through the weeds and grasses in the ditch.

—Jake! Shelly yelled. It's a duster!

He kept pedaling into the red, and then he was gone and red sand pelted our windshield and filled the air and the space between him and us. Shelly yelled again.

—Roll up your window, I said to her.

She found the handle and double-armed it closed. I rolled up mine and pulled the truck over.

—You keep that door shut, I told her.

An open spot in the wind blew by and I saw Jake lying beside his bike in the ditch. A gust had knocked him over. The open spot passed and Jake disappeared again.

I jumped out of the truck and the door slammed behind me. Another gust came up and threw me against the grille of the truck. Shelly screamed. I pushed myself off the grille and ran down into the ditch. My lungs filled with dust and my feet hit the edge of the road and stumbled into the grasses of the ditch. I landed on my knees and rolled and covered my eyes with my forearm. I got up and ran forward and tripped over the bike. My hands felt around for Jake but he wasn't there. His cap flew past me. I buried my nose and mouth into the corner of my arm again and got up and ran into the wind. The dirt and sand hammered my ears. Jake appeared a step in front of me and I swiped at him to pick him up but missed. I kept going, dust pelting off my chest, stinging my arms. He appeared again and I lunged and brought him down. We struggled on the ground and my arms folded around him. He stayed tense and ready to bolt if my grip loosened. I wrapped my two arms around him more tightly and put my back against the wind. Another lull in the gusts came through and he struggled to get free. I squeezed him tighter until he stopped heeling me in the shins. The lull ended and I closed my eyes again against the dust that whipped around us.

—Stay still, I yelled.

I thought about which way the road was and which direction the truck would be once I found asphalt.

—The next break we're running to the truck, I told him, my voice loud and in his ear. Dust and small rocks struck the back of my neck. The boy didn't acknowledge what I'd said. Maybe he hadn't heard. A slight break in the wind passed over us and I pulled the boy up, grabbing him with one arm and shielding my eyes with the other. The truck appeared briefly and was washed out again by another gust that bent me forward. I stumbled and both Jake and I hit the ground. I held him there in the grasses, waiting for our next chance to get up and get to the truck. I put a hand to Jake's eyes to shield them from the rocks flying through the air. Another lull came and I pulled us up and took a step toward the road, my eyes closed. I took another and felt the beginning of the ditch's incline. The wind nearly brought us down again. I felt asphalt under my feet and then the rumble strip, and I turned us toward where the truck would be, the wind pushing me from behind, my body protecting Jake's. I used the grooves of the rumble strip to brace myself against the wind. I kept my eyes closed and trusted I hadn't yet passed the truck.

I was pushed against the truck before I saw it, Jake pinned between the grille and me. Another screech from Shelly came through the windshield as we were pressed over the hood. I stepped to the side of the truck and grabbed the door handle as another gust tried to push us past it. I opened the door and threw Jake in, then I pressed against the door again to win space for myself to climb into the cab. My feet cleared the threshold and the wind slammed the door behind me.

The three of us sat, breathing hard through our noses, waiting for the dust in the cab to settle to the floor. I put my hands to my eyes until they started to water and then gently began trying to clear the red soil from them. I looked into the rearview and saw red tracks running down the sides of my face.

—You okay? my niece asked me.

I shook the end of my T-shirt out and started to dab the red from the corners of my eyes.

—You okay? I asked her. I stopped trying to clean my eyes and waited for more tears to form.

—Where's the bottle of water? my niece asked.

—We need that for drinking.

—You need to see, she said.

—Get the reservoir water, I said.

I heard her bending down to run her hand under the seat.

—Here. She pressed the bottle into my arm.

Only a few ounces remained in this bottle. I tipped my head back and first poured drops of water over my closed eyes, then tried to open them, pouring a little more. I blinked, waiting until the floaters fell to the sides. My vision was tinted red. Jake sat beside me with his face in his palms, not moving.

—Hey, I said.

He didn't move.

—Put your hands down, I told him.

The wind rocked the truck left and right. When the gusts came up strong, the grille of the truck rattled and whistles came from the wind, ripping past our doors. The radio antenna knocked against the windshield.

—Put your hands down, I told him again. My eyelids still wanted to close. I blinked them hard again and forced them open.

Shelly reached over and gently pulled Jake's hands from his face. He didn't resist. I poured a small amount of water in my palm and leaned his face into it. I tried to run it over both eyes. Red water flowed through my fingers and down onto Jake's pants. I repeated this until Jake's hands pressed mine away and he delicately worked the corners of his eyes with his own fingers, softly pushing the muddy water out and across his cheeks. His eyes opened and he stared at the watermarks on his jeans. He closed his eyes and waited a moment. He brought his eyes back open. I tossed the empty bottle to Shelly's feet.

—You want some water? I asked him. To drink?

Shelly held the bottle from the bar under his face so he could see it. He shook his head.

—You want some? I said to Shelly.

She shook her head too.

—You're not thirsty?

—Yeah, I'm thirsty.

—You have to drink some water, I said. Just drink a little.

—No.

—You have to drink something. It's too hot out here not to.

She reached over and took the bottle from me.

—Only if you drink too, she said.

—Okay.

She tipped the bottle back and two swallows went down.

—That's good, I said.

She wiped the drips from her mouth.

—How is it?

—It's okay, she said. Your turn. She handed the bottle back to me.

I took two gulps like she had and put the cap back on. I swallowed dirt and dust along with the water.

—It's not that good, I said.

Shelly shook her head.

Jake looked up over the dashboard. He pushed himself back in the seat with his hands, then got to his knees and spun around to look out the back window of the cab. I looked through the rearview to see what had caught his attention. Nothing was visible, just lines of red dust blowing away from us. I turned back around. The redness ran up against the windshield and the wind rocked the truck and a steady stream of tears brought more red out of our eyes and down our cheeks.

—This is a big one, Shelly said. We watched clouds of red pummel the windshield.

—Yeah, I said.

—You can't see anything, she said.

—Nope.

And then the racket the dust was making on the windshield lessened and the truck stopped being buffeted back and forth. The white of the sun began to edge through the red dust. A moment after that the wind stopped and a strong buzzing in my ears replaced all the other sounds that had been pounding against the truck.

—Stay here, I told Shelly and Jake.

I opened my door and stepped outside. Dunes of dirt ringed the backside of each tire. A bank of dust covered the bottom half of the windshield. I cupped the dust in my hand and swept it off the side of the hood.

At the edge of the ditch, I looked for Jake's bike. All the grasses were pushed over. They weren't springing back. The bike lay under some of these grasses, every blade of grass and each part of the bike covered in a cap of red. I walked to the bike and picked it up and the red dust slid off of it. Blue emerged from underneath. I carried the small bike back and lifted it into the bed of the truck. I opened the door and got back in the cab.

—I couldn't find your hat, I told Jake.

He was facing forward now. He kept still and silent. Shelly shook her dress up and down and dust alighted from it and I told her not to do that.

—Sorry, she said.

—It's fine, I said. We'll shake everything out once we get going again.

—Can I open my window? It's hot, she said.

—Of course.

Shelly was right. The heat had come back. The air was still now. The sun was beating down again. I could feel sweat beginning to run down my back.

—Why are these dumps here? Shelly asked, looking up to where the mine tailings were visible now, the red clouds having begun to fall back to the ground.

—It's the leftovers of what they pulled from the mines.

—And they piled it all here?

—Yeah. They put all the tailings there. Now they're taking it back up to the plant.

—Up where?

—Back up in the mountains.

—Why?

—They have new processes now. They can get more stuff out of them now.

—More gold?

—No, I said. Iron, I think. Titanium.

I rolled down my window and a small breeze passed over the three of us, sitting and sweating in the truck. Jake fixed his eyes on the keys swaying slightly from the ignition. There were bits of rocks in my eyes that had yet to be flushed out. I blinked slowly.

—We're going up to the dumps, I said to him. He glanced at me and out the back window then turned forward again and pushed himself up in the seat. He shrugged his shoulders and nodded. The dumps were better than whatever he'd been running from.

—What are you worried about? Shelly asked him.

He brought a big breath in and quickly let it out and fiddled with his band. He was blue, same as me. He spun it twice and put his hands on his thighs, as if to help keep them still.

—He always so quiet? I asked Shelly.

94

She shook her head.

—He's in your grade? I asked her.

—Yeah. We sit by each other. Or sat by each other. Last year.

—And he talked a lot in school?

She nodded her head again.

A remnant gust from the storm buffeted the truck lightly and we rocked left to right. Jake came out of his trance and looked up through the windshield.

I started the engine and brought the column to drive but kept my foot on the brake.

—You can get back on your bike and keep going wherever you were going, I said to Jake, although I wouldn't have let him go.

He kept quiet and still, then he looked for a moment at my blue band. He pushed himself up and looked back at his bike in the bed of the truck. He turned back around and sat with his hands tucked underneath his butt.

Shelly reached down to her feet where the skull had fallen and lifted it back to her lap. Jake turned his head toward it and then turned toward me and this time our eyes met and he looked forward again. He rocked once left and then right, adjusting his hands, which he was still sitting on.

—I think he's staying, Shelly said.

—Okay, I said.

I turned the key to the ignition but the truck was already on and it screeched and Jake jumped at the grinding noise.

—Sorry, I said to him.

He just kept looking ahead, down the road.

—To the dumps, then, I said.

—Why there? Shelly said. She coughed and put a hand over her mouth as convulsions moved through her body. She pulled the skull tightly to her with the other hand. She coughed for a moment more and then squeezed the ratcheting out of her core. I waited.

—You good? I asked.

She bent over and grabbed a magazine from her feet and ripped out a page and wiped dark phlegm from the corner of her mouth and her hand.

—I have a friend there. He might be able to tell us what Phillip couldn't.

She nodded her head, swallowing hard past the scratches in her throat. To the dumps, she said.

She tossed the magazine and phlegm-covered page down to her feet with the empty plastic bottle. I pulled the truck onto the highway. Red drifts of dust lay across the asphalt and the truck flowed through them, the knobs of the tires going silent and then returning once they were on bare asphalt again. Air came through our windows and took dust that had accumulated on the dashboard and in our clothes and flung it out to where it had come from. Jake pulled his hands out from under him and snapped his T-shirt out from his chest and dust spilled from it and rose into the air. He closed his eyes as the dust whirled away.

The mine tailings sat calm and flat now, a hundred yards ahead, lying in a thick line of red between us and where the brown foothills started. Mining rigs hauled the red tailings across the edge of the plains and back up into the foothills. Empty rigs came in from the south, their tailgates banging loosely as their drivers geared low to climb the incline back into the piles of tailings. We arrived at an intersection and I pulled the truck to a stop. I couldn't hear the tailgates banging against the backs of the rigs, I could only see them, and maybe I felt the concussions they sent across the empty space between us and them, open grassland with no grass. Grasslessland. Maybe the concussions vibrated through our cracked windshield, moving through each particle of dust that still hovered in the air. And if I felt these concussions, as little as they were, whatever they were, I knew my niece and her friend felt them, their little bodies perched on the bench seat of the old truck, looking out and watching the big trucks, wondering what those tailgates swinging loosely from the backs of those trucks would sound like up close.

—What are you waiting for? Shelly asked.

I looked at her, wondering what she was talking about.

—Are you going to go? she asked.

Another rig pulled up the incline into the dump. Its tailgate flapped open and closed and opened again, swinging with force from its upper hinges.

—Can you hear that? I asked.

—Hear what? Shelly asked.

—The tailgate. When it bangs against the back of the truck like that.

—The empty trucks?

I nodded. She waited. Listened. Jake tapped his feet together.

—Shh, Shelly said to him.

His feet stilled. She waited some more.

—No, she said.

—Yeah, me neither, I said.

We sat a moment more.

—It feels like I can hear it though, Shelly said.

—Yeah, me too, I said.

Jake sat quietly.

—Should we be able to hear it? Shelly asked.

—No, probably not. Too far away still, I guess.

Shelly nodded her head.

Another car stopped at the four-way intersection. I waved them through. They drove in front of us and away. I looked both ways again, glanced in my mirrors, and drove through the intersection toward the dumps. Jake took the skull from Shelly and held it on his lap. He turned it around to look at its backside and then turned it to face him. He turned it back to face forward again. Shelly watched Jake's hands. Jake was looking forward out the windshield again, but his hands were flaking dirt that Shelly somehow hadn't found off the skull. Some of the dust was swept up and into the breezes coming through the cab; some settled into the folds of his jeans.

—What's that? Shelly asked him.

He looked down at his hands, where his thumbs were passing over the back of the skull.

—Looks like a dent, Shelly said.

Jake's thumbs ran through an indentation behind where the left ear had been. He moved his thumbs away and the depression was clear. Jake tilted the skull up so we could look at the area more closely. We crested another hill and the mountains of red tailings were in front of us now, the clanging of the tailgates audible through the dust and hot air.

—What's that part called? Shelly asked, pointing to where Jake's fingers had been.

—The mastoid portion, I said.

—Mastoid, she said.

—Yep.

—Portion.

I nodded.

—How do you get a dent in your mastoid portion? Shelly asked.

I thought of what I might say to get around this. And then I saw that Shelly knew there was no good reason for a dent to be in the back of the girl's head. Jake set the skull carefully between them.

—I'm glad we have her with us, Shelly said.

—Yeah, me too, I said.

At the entrance to the dumps a braided steel cord hung loosely from one post to another. A man stood by one of the posts and dropped the cord to the ground to let a big dump truck pass by. We waited across the intersection from the entrance. A line of smaller trucks followed the rig up the incline, the type of trucks we'd seen back at the reservoir, enforcer trucks. Five or six total. The first one had its lights flashing and the ones that followed had the firepower: gunmen standing up in the beds of the pickups, some leaning over the cabs with their rifles ready in their hands, others with their rifles slung over their backs.

—Don't look at them, I told Shelly and Jake. They looked straight ahead, trying not to peek. Don't look, I said again.

The gunners wore masks and bandanas over their faces. Flashes of sunshine glimmered off their glasses. The man in charge of the entrance watched the last truck climb the incline into the tailings and reached down and picked up the cord and hooked it to its post. He looked over at us, waiting across the road. I pulled through the intersection but headed north. The man watched us for a moment as we passed him and then he turned back and concentrated on the next rig that was headed toward him.

—We're not going up there? Shelly said.

—Not anymore, I said.

—Why not?

—Didn't look like a good time to be there.

—Whose side were they on? Shelly asked.

—Doesn't matter, I said.

—But you know.

—I have an idea. A buzzing came from her side of the truck. The phone, I said. In your backpack.

She bent forward and brought her pack to her lap and started running her hands through the pockets. The buzzing stopped. Her hand found the phone.

—Message from Mom, she said.

—What's it say? I asked.

—Says, "Where are you?" What should I say?

—Tell her we're safe.

Shelly looked back south, toward Conrad and the layer of red dust hanging over it.

—I'll ask her if there's dust from the duster down there, she said.

—You're answering a question with a question?

—Yeah. She typed in the message and pressed send. The phone buzzed again. That was quick, Shelly said.

—What's it say?

—"Where are you?"

—See? I said.

—Hmm, Shelly said.

—What are you going to say?

Jake leaned over to have a look at the message. Shelly pressed reply and started keying in her response.

—I'll just tell her the truth, she said.

—That's perfect, I said.

She brought the phone closer to her face to see the letters below the numbers.

—Where are your glasses? I said.

—In my backpack.

—You should put them on.

—They don't help much for this stuff, she said, which was true, she was nearsighted.

—Can you see the letters?

She held the phone closer to her eyes and squinted.

—Yeah, she said.

Jake watched her thumb in her message.

—There, she said.

—Send another and tell her you love her.

—Did that.

—You're a fast typer.

She flipped the phone shut and put it in the chest pocket of her dress.

—What else did you tell her?

—That we were at the dumps, Shelly said.

—She won't like that, I said.

—Nope.

—Did you tell her where we were going?

—I don't know where we're going.

—True, I said. But where did we go the last time we were up here?

—To get the sweetwater, she said.

—That's right.

—Really? Can we? Shelly said, excited.

I nodded.

—You think there's some left? The gashouse guy said there was none left.

—He doesn't know our spot, I said.

She bounced her back against her seat and smiled and almost let out a giggle. She reached into her chest pocket and pulled out the phone again and started typing. My niece had seen so much, and yet she was somehow still a kid, with a kid's ability to kick her heels against the floor of the truck when she was excited. She pressed send and flipped the phone shut.

—Mom can't be mad about us going to get sweetwater, she said, smiling.

Maybe it was the adventure clothes that protected her, or the back-pack full of adventure stuff. She bent forward and ran her hand on the floor of the truck and came up with an empty plastic bottle in her hands. She threaded and unthreaded its top, she squinted through the windshield. She was ready for her sweetwater.

12   We headed alongside the massive eastern wall of mine tailings extending north. Plants I didn't recognize grew up the sides of this wall, they were chalk colored, dusty white, with only hints of green. This dull green, a sick green, was the only indication that these plants were alive, as though they were very nearly something other than plants, something able to live off of the heavy metals that sat within these mine tailings. It was as though a fourth branch of living creatures had been created, swaying stiffly and awkwardly in the breezes created by the rigs that drove by them, these fake breezes pushing these fake creatures back and forth in short, rigid motions. These creatures covered the hillside, and as we reached the end of the tailings, these creatures ended too, and the land returned to its flat emptiness, with only the rare ragged sage brush swaying in the fake breezes made by our truck and the rigs, swaying only slightly less rigidly, and growing only shades less of the sickly green, as though they were, in fact, ghosts of plants that had come before, sent to populate the flatness and the sparseness and to be the only reminder of life that had once flourished here. They were ghosts in a land no longer able to support living creatures as we had known them, creatures that this land had begun squeezing out long ago.

—You should slow down, Shelly said. I checked the speedometer but it had been broken since I had learned to drive. Its needle bounced on the peg that kept it from falling below five miles per hour. I let off the gas and we rounded a curve and the right wheels snapped over the rumble strips until I could bring the truck fully back into our lane.

—I can't wait for that water, I said.

—Me either, Shelly said.

Pumpjacks and flares replaced the mountains of red tailings and I listened to the whinnying of the horse heads as we neared the spring. The entrance to the sweetwater wasn't far, but it wasn't obvious—just a small hitch in the barbed-wire fence line that bordered the right side of the highway. We passed a mile marker, but the mileage was unreadable.

—Was that the marker for the entrance? I asked Shelly.

—I don't know. She turned around to look at it.

—Me either. You know what we're looking for, right? I said to Shelly. She turned back around.

—Yeah. Mile 56. But I won't be able to see the 56. She giggled. Then after that the telephone pole with the reflector on it.

—Yep.

—But I think we need to get closer to the butte, she said. And that was right. We were going to hike up the butte to find the spring. It wasn't worth looking for the hidden entrance until we were almost alongside the butte.

—Do you think Jake has been to the spring? Shelly asked.

—You been to the spring, Jake? I asked him.

He didn't hear me. I asked him again. He broke his stare out the windshield and looked at me. He shook his head.

—Doesn't look like it, I said to Shelly.

She watched a telephone pole pass by on the right. She watched it go by and then looked up to watch the next one.

—You're not going to believe the spring, Jake, Shelly said. She watched another telephone pole go by and looked ahead for the next one.

—Does Jen know those guys? Shelly said.

—Know what guys?

—Those guys in the trucks. The ones who went up into the dumps.

—Jen works with those guys, yeah, I said.

—Jen's on their side? she said.

—Jen doesn't have a side. Like us.

—But she used to have a side. Like us, Shelly said.

—A ways back, yeah, that's right.

—But not anymore.

—Not anymore, I said.

Shelly's red tennis shoes touched the dashboard. She tried to rest them there but her legs weren't quite long enough. The floppy bottoms of her shoes wouldn't grip.

—How did Jen get out, Shelly asked.

—They took someone from her.

—Who'd they take from her?

—They took her brother.

—There it is! Shelly said.

The telephone pole with the reflector passed by, then the break in the fence passed by. We had missed the mile marker. I looked in the mirror and nobody was coming. I backed up the truck and pulled it through the ditch until the front bumper was touching the loose wires of the barbed-wire fence.

—You remember how to undo the gate? I asked her.

—Yep! and she was out the door and onto the ground. She ran to the side of the gate with the sistered posts and she hugged them one to the other until there was enough slack in the loop to push the loop up and away. She dragged the gate's three rusted wires aside and I drove through.

In the rearview mirror I watched her pull the loose post back into place. She stuck the base of the post into the bottom loop and propped it up a few inches with her toe. Jake sat on his knees, watching Shelly work, following each step she took. Her feet gripped the loose soil and her body tilted into the top of the post, pushing it tightly against the other, and then she flipped the top loop down and let go of the post and it sprang back, taut, and was held shut.

Shelly ran back to her door and opened it and jumped into the cab. Jake was smiling.

—Good work, I said.

—Let's go. Shelly pulled her hair out of her face and tucked it behind her ears. She coughed again, letting out what she had suppressed while working the gate, and looked ahead to the butte and waited for me to step on the gas to get the truck moving. I put the truck in drive and started in through the dry bunchgrass and sage, heading up the slope. Jake held the skull tightly in his lap and he and Shelly rocked back and forth. I picked our way between boulders and patches of dead brush. I headed to a gully lined with scrub and dry juniper. I brought the truck through a shallow part and then headed up the hill as far as I could and parked behind a clump of thickets. We were hidden from the road. I wasn't sure if we needed to be hidden. It felt like we did.

—Ready to walk a bit? I asked Jake and Shelly.

Shelly opened her door and gravity pulled her so she slid off the seat and out of the truck. She landed and took a few steps down the incline and then watched Jake scoot over the seat toward her. He grasped the skull in his left arm and inched toward the door and then let gravity do the same to him. He landed on his feet and bent over and took a few steps to stop his momentum like Shelly had.

—Nice jump, Shelly said. She swung the door to shut it but it didn't quite make it. It swung back to her and she got a better grip on it and swung it harder so it made it up the angle on which it pivoted. The latch clicked shut.

—You have your backpack? I asked her.

—Shoot.

She stepped back to the door and opened it and let it swing open and its weight shoved her backward but she kept her footing and steadied herself. Jake moved out of the way so the door wouldn't hit him.

I opened my door and climbed out. I leaned back into the truck and over the seat and shoveled the empty water containers out Shelly's door as she grabbed her backpack. They fell out of the truck and Jake picked them up from the ground. I flipped the back of the bench seat forward and found a few more plastic bottles we could collect water with.

—Where's the big container? I asked.

Shelly slammed her door again and came around to my side of the truck. She put her foot on the rear tire and pulled herself up to have a look in the truck bed.

—There it is, she said.

—Grab it.

She stepped around the cooler that held the bones of the girl to where the container lay in the far corner. She picked it up and tossed it to Jake. She came back across the bed and got down the way she'd climbed up.

—Anything that can hold water, bring, I said. I opened the hood of the truck and pulled the distributor cap.

—Yeah, she said, her voice clear, excited. She pulled herself back up on the tire to take one more look into the bed of the truck. Nothing else!

—Okay. I slammed the hood shut and flipped the cap to Shelly.

She caught it and jumped to the ground and ran around to the downhill side of the truck and started taking the bottles from Jake's hands and loading up her backpack. She put the cap in last and zipped the pack shut and swung it on. She nodded to me.

—I'm so thirsty, she said.

—Yeah, me too. Let's go, I said.

13 Shelly headed up the hill toward the butte. Her yellow dress caught on bushes and yucca as she walked by them, but she ignored all these things. She walked right through them. Didn't notice the snags and the tugs at her clothes. Jake followed her and I followed Jake. He had the skull tucked under his arm. Rocks spun away from the bottoms of Shelly's tennis shoes as she pushed herself forward. She paused briefly at moments to look for the best way up the steep parts. She looked behind her to see if we were keeping up.

We crested the steepest part of the slope and came to a false summit and then shortly afterward came to the final gradual climb to the flat top of the butte, where we walked for a hundred yards more, each of us following our own path now, picking our individual way through the bunch grasses, larger and more numerous than their cousins on the valley floor.

—There it is, my niece said, and skipped a couple of steps, like a kid on a playground. She returned to a walk, but a faster version of a walk now. Jake looked over at me. I pointed up ahead.

—The clump of trees, I said to him. Up there.

A slight decline took us down the north-facing slope of the butte. Jake looked to where I pointed and then put his head back down and concentrated on threading his way through the scrubland.

My niece arrived at the stand of trees, more a forest than a stand, and sidestepped through a narrow opening between green pine boughs. Jake and I took the same path as Shelly, following her into the shade and coolness and onto the moist, dark soil. She took us through the trees, past the fir needles, almost cold to the touch, and soft, soft needles, only scraping us lightly. Shelly stopped and Jake and I stopped behind her. She looked back at us and then up ahead and to our sides. I couldn't tell if she was getting her bearings, wondering which way to turn, or resting her lungs—or just stopping to breathe in the fresh air. Her chest moved smoothly, without a hitch. She took in a deep breath and smiled at me.

—You know the way? I asked her. She nodded.

Shelly led us farther into the forest and then as light between the trees began to appear she led us to this light. We came out of the forest at a clearing and she paused for a moment at this line between trees and prairie and the straps of her backpack heaved up and fell down in full, healthy breaths. Her thumbs hooked into the straps and she looked left and right down the tree line.

—Left, I said.

She leaned forward and looked right down the border of the trees, making sure I was correct, and then turned and continued leading us left, alongside the trees. We rounded a slight bend in the tree line and Shelly saw the boulder she was looking for and again skip-jumped out of her walk and yelled at us to hurry and she started running, her pack bouncing off the small of her back with each stride. Jake tried to keep up, jumping over the shorter bushes rather than running around them. Shelly was fast. I couldn't remember the last time I'd seen her run.

Jake and Shelly disappeared behind the boulder and I started running too. I jumped over what I could and ran through what wouldn't trip me. I came to the other side of the boulder and they were both on their knees with their mouths in the small pool of water that flowed up from somewhere beneath the boulder.

—Is it still good? I asked. I was out of breath.

—Yeah, Shelly said, and she choked on her water and coughed and giggled and turned to spit out what hadn't gone down right and took several big breaths and coughs to clear the water she'd swallowed too quickly. She laughed at herself. Jake came up from the water and swallowed and laughed too. Shelly kept laughing as she undid the straps of her backpack and set it beside her and unzipped the large compartment and began taking out the plastic bottles. The front of her yellow dress floated loosely in the water in front of her knees.

—Isn't the water good? she said to Jake.

He nodded and went back to the water, his head and mouth sending ripples across the small pool.

Shelly held out a water bottle for me to fill. I stepped up to her and took it.

—You gotta get some, she said to me.

I kneeled and unscrewed the cap of the bottle. It had been crushed a bit and I blew into it to flex it out. It crinkled and popped and unfolded and I dipped it, bottom first, into the water and slowly let the mouth go below the surface. The water flowed into the bottle and I pushed the bottom deeper so that more water could flow in. The pool was shallow, no deeper than the bottle standing straight. A small creek, not even a creek, a seep, ran out the back of the pool and into the green grasses and green sages that lived on this gentle slope of the north side of the butte. The trickle of water ended somewhere within the sage. The slope ended a hundred yards on at a cliff, a series of crags that fell back to the prairie floor that continued north. We all kneeled, shoulder to shoulder and knee to knee, and filled the bottles with the sweetwater. I took the bottle of water I'd gotten at the bar and dumped it out and washed it with the sweetwater and then filled it up.

—There's less than last time, Shelly said.

—Yeah, I said.

I lifted my bottle and emptied it into my mouth.

—We have to bring enough back for Mom and Grandpa and Grandma.

—Yep, I said.

She grabbed the five-gallon container and started filling it, filling a small bottle and then dumping it into the container and then filling it again, taking gulps for herself in between. I gulped down another bottle full of sweetwater and then helped her fill the container.

—So good, right? Shelly said, smiling up at me.

—So good, I said. And so cold.

We filled our bottles and went to the boulder and sat with our backs to its shaded cool surface and looked out over the valley that spread up to the north and we looked over at the mountains that came into this valley from the west and lifted it up and out of the brown layer of soot that covered most of it. I put my head back against the boulder and drank more water.

—How many can you count? Shelly asked.

I opened my eyes and finished swallowing the sweetwater I had been holding in my mouth, cold like the granite boulder we leaned against, and I started counting on the highest part of the alluvial plain that sat like a wedge between the mountains and the plains. There was a group of pumpjacks on the highest reaches of the slope and I started counting there. I noticed Shelly had decided to start from the most eastern point in the plains where pumpjacks could still be seen.

—We're counting the oil horses, Shelly told Jake.

He pulled his shoes underneath him and started a count of his own. Shelly leaned in and squinted her eyes and put an index finger in front of her face to track each one she numbered.

—Where are your glasses? I asked her.

She stopped counting and reached for her backpack and opened the outside pocket and after pushing some things around pulled out her dusty spectacles. I stopped counting too.

—Let me see those, I said.

She handed them to me and I poured a splash of water over the lenses and worked the end of my T-shirt through the water and dust and then repeated the process. I held them up to the sky and they were clean but full of scratches. She had a string tied from hinge to hinge that made do for the absence of arms.

—We need to get you some new ones, I said.

Shelly giggled and took them from my hand.

—That's what you always say, she said. She put them on and adjusted the string around the back of her head and around her ears and teetered them back and forth on her nose until they were where she wanted them. She looked back up to the flat stretch of prairie to the east and began her count again. She stopped, though, and nodded her head slightly up and down, finding the clear spot in her lenses between the scratches.

—There are so many more, she said.

—With your glasses on? I said.

She giggled.

—Yeah, but there's just more.

—Yeah, I said.

She tilted her head forward and moved her glasses down the curve of her nose until her eyes weren't looking through the glasses anymore, then she tilted her head back again to look through the lenses. She teetered like this twice more.

—The glasses definitely still help, she said.

—One hundred twenty-four, Jake said.

Shelly and I looked at him.

—What? I said.

Jake tried to speak again but he couldn't. The number had come out in spite of himself.

—He said one hundred twenty-four, Shelly said.

Jake nodded.

—Wow, I said.

—There were only . . . how many were there last time? Shelly asked.

—Fifty-seven, I think.

Shelly adjusted her glasses again and started her count once more. I turned to the clump of pumpjacks in the west.

—Every one, right? Shelly asked. Not just the ones that are active?

—Every one, I said.

We each made our way, counting, across the plains that lay before us, Shelly giggling when we crossed paths somewhere in the middle and were counting the same horses. In a few moments more I was done.

—Wait, don't say anything, she said.

She redoubled her concentration and her index finger put the final count on the last pumpjacks. Her shoulders relaxed and she murmured her number to herself a few times. I couldn't hear it. She scanned back across from where she had started counting. She took her glasses off and hung them by their string over her forearm. Her shoulders relaxed again after a deep breath in and she weighed her number one more time against what she saw in front of her. We both smiled.

—Ready? she said.

—Yes.

She began a count to three.

—One, two, three . . .

We both said our numbers—one hundred twenty for me and one hundred twenty-eight for her.

—Wait, what was yours? she asked.

—One hundred twenty, I said.

—Jake! You were right in the middle, she said.

Jake smiled and untucked his feet from underneath himself and hit the backs of his knees against the ground two or three times and then pulled his feet back near him, crossing one over the other.

—That's a lot, Shelly said.

—Yep.

—When was the last time we were up here? she asked.

—Six months? No. Maybe a year ago? I don't know.

Shelly squinted over the flat land and took in the sight.

—I bet it's pretty at night, with all these flames burning, she said.

—Yeah, you're probably right, I said.

—Dangerous though, right?

—Yeah, it could be dangerous, I said. Day or night.

—Yeah.

She slid her glasses from her forearm and stuffed them in her backpack where she had found them.

—You don't have a case for those? I asked.

She giggled again and didn't respond and went back to looking out over the plains.

—You should keep those on more, I said.

—I need a new string for them. She started giggling again at the ridiculousness of what she'd said. I tried to keep a straight face at this but couldn't and she saw that she'd made me smile and she started to laugh. She was a funny kid. She leaned forward to where Jake had placed the skull and pulled it toward her, her laughter falling off. She set it on the ground in front of her, counterbalancing it with a tuft of bunch grass so that its eyes had a level view over the plains.

—I bet she likes the view, I said.

—Yep, Shelly said and giggled a bit more and smiled big, like she hadn't smiled in a while, and looked at me and then let her giggle turn into a laugh again. I giggled a bit too, and then she laughed more because I was giggling and she had probably never seen me giggle before.

—What time is it? I asked her, trying to recover my seriousness.

Her laughing stopped but her giggling continued. She took her watch face out of her chest pocket, continuing to smile. She picked up her bottle of water with her free hand and tried to relax her giggling so she could take a drink. Her head tilted back and she took a couple of more swigs and then wiped her arm across her mouth and caught her breath. She glanced at the watch and put it back in her pocket.

—Five o'clock, she said. She leaned her water bottle up against the skull. She uncrossed her legs and shook them out like Jake had, their backs slapping against the ground. Her dress bounced and made a wave with each movement of her legs.

—I've never been out there, she said.

—Out where? I said.

—Out there, north. Past that point of revision out there. She pointed to the buildings and vehicles on the highway that formed the barricade. There were small dots of people walking to and from the buildings and trucks. Browning sat north and to the west and Cut Bank north and to the east. A highway ran through the plains and the pumpjacks that sat between them.

—You sure you haven't been up past there? I said.

She nodded. Drops of sweetwater hung from her chin.

—Sure, she said. She brought her hand over her chin and wiped away the drops.

—They look like a bunch of bison walking around, she said.

—The horseheads?

—Yeah, she said.

—Yeah.

—A big growing herd of bison walking all the way to the Line, she said.

—What do you think they do at the Line? I asked.

—Like once they're at the crossing?

—Yeah.

—They just walk on over it, she said.

—I bet they do, I said.

—Can't stop a bison when it's set its mind on something.

—True. And then what do they do?

She leaned forward with her elbows on her knees then she let her knees drop and sat cross-legged, like Jake. She patted down her dress and spun her fingers through the laces of her shoes.

—Once they're across the Line? she asked.

—Yeah. Once they're past the barriers.

She pulled her feet against herself and leaned forward. Her eyes squinted more tightly until a few lines formed at their corners.

—Can you see all the way across the Line? I asked her.

—Almost, she said.

—Maybe with your glasses?

She smiled and let the lines fall from her face and she leaned back. Whatever she had seen through her squinted eyes had satisfied her.

—I think they drink all the sweetwater they want, she said. It's everywhere up there. And then after that I have no idea what they do. Sleep with a bellyful of sweetwater, probably.

Her back rested against the boulder as she looked over the plains toward the Northern Line, then she leaned her head back too, softly laying it against the boulder's lichen-covered face. She closed her eyes and the lines in their corners faded completely away. She giggled again, maybe thinking of happy bison with bellyfuls of sweetwater, or the new string she'd get for her glasses someday.

—When was the last time you were up there? she asked, her eyes still closed.

—I've never been across the Line, I said.

—But up past those towns.

—Up past Browning and Cut Bank?

She didn't nod or say yeah or give any sign that she had heard what I had asked. She just sat there, resting against the cool granite, her chest moving freely up and down, breathing deeply and smoothly through her nose. The hem of her yellow dress lay frayed and dirty on the ground. The treads of her red tennis shoes were coming off at the heels. The tops of her forearms—crossed over her stomach, moving away from her and back again with her quiet breaths—had thin red scratches on them from breaking trail through the pine boughs. She was a beautiful kid on the Front, having a great adventure in the hills outside of town.

—What's that smell? she asked, eyes still closed.

I took in a breath through my nose. Jake did the same. He looked around, trying to put an object to it, trying to source it. He couldn't. I exhaled and took another breath. It was sap. The pine trees. It was the smell of damp forest. I hadn't placed it right away.

—It's the pine trees, I told her.

Jake leaned forward and looked at the line of evergreens running across the slope. Shelly kept her eyes closed. She smiled.

—Wow, she said. I guess I didn't remember that from last time.

—Me either, I said.

She filled up with this pine tree air again, her lungs working smoothly, pulling as much as she could through her nose. Her back arched away from the rock and then fell back to its contour as she exhaled.

—Oh my gosh. It smells so amazing, she said. Her eyes slowly opened. She bent her head back, looking at the pine boughs that stretched over the granite boulder and above our heads. She bent forward and reached for her water bottle leaning against the skull. She unscrewed the cap and took a long drink, finishing it.

—Can I have the rest of yours? she asked.

I tossed my bottle to her and she caught it cleanly and unscrewed the cap. She took a big swig and handed the bottle to Jake. He finished it.

—What was that one story? Shelly asked, watching Jake finish the water.

—Which one? I said.

—The bison one. She panned her head back and forth across the plain. The one with the storm, she said. Shelly and Jake looked at me.

—Oh, I said, vaguely remembering something about a bison.

Shelly kept looking at me. What was it? she said.

—It's not a story.

—Well, what is it? she asked.

I looked out at all the pumpjacks below us.

—I don't know, I said. It's more like a lesson. Nothing happens.

—But what happens? There's bison and there's a storm, she said.

I tried to think of it.

—It's just that when there's a storm coming, bison will turn and face into it.

—They'll face into the storm, she said.

—Yeah, I said. Most other animals will walk away from the storm, their backs to it.

—Bison will walk into it, she said.

—That's right. You get through the storm faster if you confront it, walk toward it.

—That's the lesson? she asked. Walk into the storm.

—I think so, yeah, I said.

Shelly and Jake looked back out over the plain and at the bison pumpjacks bobbing their heads up and down.

—That makes sense, she said.

—Yep, I said.

She kept staring at the bison down on the plain.

—They're all facing every which way, she said. Jake nodded. She was right. Some faced east, others west, some up to the Line, some south.

—Storms coming from everywhere, I guess, Shelly said.

—I guess so, I said.

She took her glasses from the pocket of her backpack and put them on again. Shelly moved the one clear spot on her glasses over the land that spread in front of us. Sometimes she stopped going left to right and tilted her head up slightly to look toward the horizon, and tilted her head down slightly to look toward the edge of the herd lining the near side of the plain. She tilted her head way back and scanned the sky for something, maybe looking for any storms coming, then returned to watching the stationary bison, each trapped facing in its own direction, facing its own individual storm.

—What's that? Shelly said, squinting out over the valley again.

—What? I said.

—The flashing.

I looked out where she was pointing and saw the flashing. It was a line of cars out east toward Cut Bank, traveling west. The lead car was large, an SUV of some kind. It had lights on its roof. Specks of red, blue, and white spun around. No sounds reached us, just light. I couldn't count the cars. Too many, and they kept coming over the eastern horizon.

—We should go, I said.

Jake was already standing up.

—Get all the bottles, I said. Fill them up again.

Shelly put her glasses away and put a hand on the boulder and pushed herself up. She picked up the bottles scattered at her feet and walked to the pool. Jake picked up the skull and slid it into Shelly's backpack.

We knelt at the pool of sweetwater and dipped the bottles below the surface, water gurgling back into them. Once they were full Shelly arranged them around the skull in her backpack. She zipped it shut.

We sat for a moment. A little moisture from the gravel and pebbles that rimmed the puddle of water we knelt at was soaking through to our knees. We watched the cars racing to the west, toward the point of revision.

—This water is so beautiful, Shelly said.

—Yeah, I said.

—We have to go? she asked.

—Yeah, I said again.

Jake nodded, his hands on his hips, his elbows wide, his face more serious than scared, his eyes focused now and not simply empty and staring. He looked at me and nodded again. I nodded back to him.

14 —Lead the way, I said to Shelly.

She looked at Jake.

—You want to lead us? she asked him.

Jake stepped in front of us and started finding our path back through the pine trees and back to the truck. We stepped through the forest's branches and smells and its scrapes, scrapes that felt more like caresses, our arms up to keep them from our eyes, the needles cool across our forearms. Everyone's step was light and quick. Shelly's red shoes hopped around the trunks of trees and pushed off the moist forest floor, and I followed each step they took through this shaded world.

We broke through the final boughs of the forest and heat knocked us back onto our heels and we all stopped and took a moment to adjust to the dust and the light and the sudden thickness of the air around us. Shelly hid her eyes in the nook of her arm. Her chest bent forward and her breath became labored, her lungs sifting through the dryness, searching how to best take in this scorched air. I moved the large container of water from one hand to another, wiping the sweat off my palms. Shelly brought her arm up over her forehead and pulled her dark hair from her face. She tried to stand straight again. She drew in a long, slow breath, forcing air to fill her little lungs.

—Let me take that, I said, reaching for her pack.

She moved her shoulder from my hand and shook her head.

—You ready? she asked me.

—Okay, I said.

—I'll lead now, she said.

Her yellow dress moved through the field of sun and burnt sage and yucca and Jake and I followed her. She floated between the snags of the bushes and she took us down her trail to our truck. Her dress ruffled around a last yucca plant and she came to the side of the pickup. She waited for me to arrive with the key to open it. I popped the door open and she slid the backpack off her shoulders and unzipped it and pulled out the distributor cap and handed it to me. I pulled the latch for the hood and walked to the front and hoisted it up and replaced the cap. I let the hood slam back into place. Shelly and Jake were in the truck waiting for me to climb in. I flipped the seat forward and put the container of water on the seat of the extra cab. Shelly grabbed the pants she'd used before and put them on the seat so that she and Jake wouldn't burn from its heat.

—Where we going now? Shelly said.

—Cut Bank.

—Isn't that where those cars were coming from? she said.

—Maybe.

A buzzing came from Shelly's backpack again. I pointed to it at her feet.

—The phone, I said.

She pulled the pack up to her lap and dug around its pockets until she found the phone.

—Mom, she said, and flipped it open. Hello? Shelly took the phone from her ear and looked at its face, trying to see if she'd opened it in time. She put it back to her ear.

—Hello?

She waited a moment, listening.

—Mom! Hey!

Shelly smiled and Jake did too and then he got to rolling down the window to let out some of the suffocating heat. Shelly pressed the phone tightly to her ear.

—Yeah, okay. Do you want to talk to him?

I held out my hand for the phone. Shelly waved it away and kept listening to her mom.

—Yep, I'll tell him, she said. She listened more. Okay, she said. I love you too. Bye.

—Wait a minute, I said. Give me the phone.

She flipped it shut.

—What did she say? I asked. What did your mom say?

—She said to go to Cut Bank.

—She did?

Shelly nodded.

—What else?

—I don't know. She just said she couldn't talk long.

—What was going on? I asked her.

—I don't know. Mom wouldn't say. They sounded like they were in a hurry.

—In a hurry. Why in a hurry?

Shelly just looked at me. She put the phone back in her backpack. Shelly didn't know.

—In a hurry, I said.

Shelly nodded.

—That's not good. I started the truck and began rolling it back down the slope to the highway.

—Stop, Shelly said.

I pressed the brake and we all leaned forward as the truck skidded lightly to a stop.

—Look, she said.

Down on the road another line of cars was speeding toward us. They had lights flashing, like the other line of cars we'd seen from on top of the butte.

—Can they see us? Shelly asked.

—If they looked, maybe.

—Would it matter if they did?

—Might. We're still kind of hidden. It probably wouldn't matter.

—We're only hidden if they don't look.

—Probably pretty hidden.

—Lots of probablies, Shelly said.

—That's right.

The line of cars kept coming around the bend we'd just traveled, and they continued over the crest of the hill, on their way to the valley where we'd counted the pumpjacks. The gap between Shelly's eyebrows narrowed. She lifted herself from the seat, pushing her fists into it to better see over the dashboard, but then sank her head between her shoulders, trying to stay hidden.

—What are you thinking? I asked her.

—What are you thinking? she asked back.

—It's all right. They won't see us. They won't come up here to bother us.

—But what were you thinking? she said.

The end of the line of cars appeared.

—Those cars are going to meet those other cars, Shelly said.

The end of the line moved over the crest of the hill. I let the footbrake up and we started rolling toward the highway.

—It's going to be a big one, I said.

—Big what? she asked.

—Big meeting.

Jake rolled his window down farther until it wouldn't go anymore. The heat in the cab made the air barely breathable. It scorched my throat as it went down. A slight breeze came over us through the open windows, but it did nothing. We needed the moving air that'd be on the road.

—Are we going to go watch the meeting? Shelly said.

I nodded.

—Go get the gate, I said.

I stopped the truck and Jake and Shelly hopped out. Jake helped Shelly move through all the steps she'd taken before. The post popped from its static twin and Shelly dragged the attached lines of barbed wires across the dried grasses. I let the truck roll through the opening and gassed it when it was at the bottom of the ditch. I pulled the truck into its lane and watched Jake and Shelly bind the gate back together. They climbed back in the truck and Jake slammed the door shut.

—Good work, guys, I said.

They slid across the bench seat until they were in their spots, ready to go. I pressed the accelerator and air came through the window and we all breathed a little easier, a little more comfortably.

—So we won't be heading back for a little bit, Shelly said.

—Not if your mom says we shouldn't.

—But we weren't for a bit anyway, right? Because of the skeleton?

—Right.

—How long you think we'll be?

—I'm not sure.

Shelly pulled off her red cap and pushed her hair together in back and pulled her red cap back on.

—A little bit later probably, I said.

—A little later probably, she repeated.

—That all right? I asked.

—Yeah, she said. We need to find out who the skeleton was first.

—That's right, I said.

I pressed the pedal further to get more air flowing through the cab.

—You sure your mom didn't say anything else?

—Not much, Shelly said.

—How much is not much?

—It's not what she said.

—More what she didn't say?

She nodded.

—Yeah, I said.

—She said they'll be all right if we're all right.

We crested the hill and all the bison we'd counted from the butte were still down in the valley, some moving, others not, but all of them black and rusting on this dried-out expanse of land, the herd a black mass that never migrated away, forever multiplying, forever appearing in the next place, until they were always everywhere, always around the next corner, always where they hadn't been before.

—We'll be all right, I said.

—So they'll be all right, she said. Mom and Grandpa and Grandma will be all right then.

—That's right, I said.

Shelly nodded firmly once. I pulled the truck over to the side of the road as the meeting was about to start. I shut the engine off and heat flooded in through the open windows.

15 Each of the bobbing heads of the bison moved at its own tempo, out of step with those around it, it was like a sea of choppy black water extending over the valley. We watched the small humans run and drive between them, finding cover behind the steel structures, pointing their rifles through the gaps of light that opened and closed between the spinwheels and the cranks and the walking beams, leaning heavily against the platforms of the rigs until a sign was given readying them for a fight. The vehicles dispersed out into the fields on each side of the point of revision, bouncing through ditches and running over dead or dying snags of sage that hadn't yet been trodden back into the ground. One by one the vehicles and the humans stopped moving. They settled in, like we had, to wait for what would happen.

A solitary volley of gunfire floated by us. And then nothing happened. We saw no movement. I couldn't tell where the shot had come from. I turned to Shelly to ask if she had heard the volley, or if perhaps I'd been mistaken. Before I could ask a retort came past us. A tentative rebuttal, followed by four more in quick succession, and then the wait was over. Down in the valley, fighters began moving from their cover, searching for somewhere better to hide, to shoot from. Others got back into their vehicles to move them, to advance them, some were put into reverse; other small human dots stopped running midstride, crumpling to the ground. All this happened while the rounded-edge volleys of gunfire floated past us, muffled in the same way our footsteps in the aqueduct had been muffled, the same way the rock we'd kicked along the river concrete had bounced hollowly in front of us. The footsteps of the runners could not be heard. Nor the throttling of the engines. There was just too much space between them and us. There was just the soft tap tap of firearms. These were the only sounds to reach us and continue past us back up the butte that stood behind us. Tap tap tap; sometimes they fell on top of each other until trying to identify individual shots wasn't possible. Sometimes they were solitary and their reverberations shook through the cracks in the windshield, the lines shimmering for an instant, vibrating, flashing over our eyes. Most commonly the recoils were evenly spaced and sounded like distant hammering, laborers pounding two-by-fours together, pauses only coming when the heads of nails sank flush with the boards.

Shelly bent to her backpack and opened the side pocket and took out her glasses. She gave them one brush with the end of her dress and pulled the string over her head and went through her process of finding an unscratched spot through which both eyes could look unencumbered at the same time. She found this spot and her head locked still. She kept her breathing shallow and smooth to keep this spot from moving from her vision. A vehicle exploded. A rocket had been fired. Shelly's head moved slightly to take in the flames that swirled into the sky, first red against brown, then black against brown, then heat waves that bent the brown into silvery ribbons, and then another explosion a hundred yards off and Shelly adjusted her head again.

Jake started grabbing at his door handle, trying to open it. There was a trick to it, a lift and then a push; he couldn't quite get it. He was frantic.

—Jake, it's okay, I said. Shelly, don't let him out.

Shelly reached over but the door popped open.

—Don't let him out, Shelly! She reached for him but he slipped away. He jumped from the seat and ran.

—Out, I told Shelly. She slid over her seat and jumped to the ground. I jumped out my side. We met at the front of the truck. Jake was running toward the meeting, out toward where the earth bent down into a slight slope that led into the valley. I had expected him to be running back toward the butte. He disappeared behind a clump of dead trees. I sent Shelly right and I made my way left. We threaded through the dead scrub that covered the hillside. If Jake kept straight, he'd have a good chance of losing us. If he swerved either way, we might have a chance of grabbing him. He was a fast kid. A scared kid. We didn't have much time for chasing. But we needed to find him. He was good to have along.

Shelly and I came to where the land bent downward toward the valley and looked out below us, she on one side of the gray trees and me on the other side. Not much cover existed between us and the battle and us and where the horseheads bobbed up and down.

—You see him? I asked Shelly.

—Where could he be? Her voice was hollow again, like the gunshots down in the valley, like our footsteps in the aqueduct. I shrugged.

—Goddammit, I said.

Shelly pointed down the slope, down toward an old red dog that limped from dead juniper to dead juniper. Jake came running out from under the only cover that was down below, the last juniper on the slope, burnt by the sun and its heat. Jake ran toward the old red dog. The dog bounced twice, up and back like a teeter-totter, then resumed its aching walk, its tail sputtered back and forth down by its heels. The dog bowed its head and its ears tucked themselves back as it pushed its way through Jake's legs and popped its head back up to look upslope at us. Its tongue was out and I could hear it whimper and whinny and it came out from under Jake and made another pass through his legs. Jake bent down and hugged its rear quarters. The dog wiggled free of Jake's embrace and went for another pass through his legs and Jake hugged him again.

—Goddammit, I said again.

Shelly started running down the slope. I walked partway and waited for them to begin walking back up. Shelly offered her hand to the dog and the dog sniffed and pushed past her hand and pushed his nose into her yellow dress and poked his nose out the other side. Shelly giggled, so did Jake. The dog sneezed and pushed its head through and then its ears popped out from under her yellow dress and they perked up at me and then it went back to Jake and made another pass between his legs. Shelly and Jake laughed; the dog let out another little sneeze.

—Come on, guys, I yelled down to them. We were out in the open. Exposed. I couldn't see the truck, hidden behind the dead junipers. The meeting continued below us. When it ended, their attention would turn toward the outskirts of the meeting, out where we were. I yelled to them. The red dog perked up its ears at me again and then looked at Jake and Jake spoke to the dog, said it was okay, said that I was okay. The three of them started walking up the slope.

The red dog walked between Shelly and Jake, Jake called him Red. Good dog, Red, and Red's tail wagged and he raised his head to both Shelly and Jake to have a look at them both and then looked up to where I stood. I reached my hand out to Red like Shelly had, but he declined to sniff and instead circled around both of them and stopped at Jake's side and sat and looked up at Jake and then up to me. The old dog's eyes were covered with gray cataracts, or perhaps calluses from too much time spent in the backs of trucks, winds blistering his corneas. None of us could have been more than a blurry shifting mass of light to him. He sat there smiling, tongue out, ears back. Tired. Suspicious of me. And thirsty. He needed water.

Jake patted Red's head.

—It's okay, Jake said, speaking more easily now. It's okay, Jake said again. I wasn't sure if he was saying it to Red or to me. An explosion drifted past us, the loudest yet to come from the meeting. Jake and Shelly turned, and so did Red, and looked down into the valley. A plume of smoke unfolded into the sky east of the point of revision. The gunfire ceased for a moment as all parties took in the sight of this black cloud rolling skyward, each person calculating what such an explosion meant to the balance of the meeting. The gunfire began anew, a sputter at first from the spaces west of the point of revision, the western party realizing the damage it had done with the rocket they'd launched, which had hit its target, and then both sides were awash again in small-arms fire, shot after shot, each closer to the one before it, like a jar of marbles poured out on a linoleum floor. The pops sped past us, louder as they did so together, in large groups, so many shots fired simultaneously. Red looked from the west to the east, as if he were taking in the meeting, a canopy of smudged browns and blacks and grays. Jake patted Red's neck, just down from his ears. Vehicles from the west slowly moved east, approaching the point of revision. Vehicles in the east began backing up, turning around. People on foot dashed from pumpjack to pumpjack. Red moved from the sunny side of Jake to his shady side, hiding from the sun. Shelly put her hand to her forehead to shade her eyes.

—Where's your hat, I asked her. She patted the top of her head, only now realizing it wasn't on.

—Must be in the truck.

—What time is it? I asked her.

She dug out the watch face from the chest pocket of her dress.

—Six, she said, and dropped the watch back into the pocket and then tilted her head left and then right to get her vision through her glasses set again.

Another billow of flames erupted to the east of the point of revision. A moment later its sound passed us, its concussion like a door slamming down a long hallway. It pushed me back onto my heels slightly.

—This one looks bigger than normal, Shelly said.

—This meeting?

—Yeah, she said.

—Yeah, I think you're right.

More people, little black dots, ran east, getting back into their cars.

—Looks like the side on the right is getting back in their cars, Shelly said.

—Those glasses really work, I said.

Shelly said yes, not nodding her head, trying to maintain the sweet spot she'd found between the scrapes on her lenses.

The cars in the east spun around in tight circles and headed back to the highway. Most didn't make it. The vehicles in the west moved in on them, continuing their pursuit, cutting their drivers down. Some eastern vehicles exploded into flames, others just stopped moving. Some drivers abandoned these static cars, firing errant shots behind them, back to the west, as they ran, before they collapsed to the ground, black dots folding flat into the dust. Movement in the west increased as movement in the east ceased. A few last discharges passed us, still no echoes, just solitary sounds, hollow sounds flowing past us, until no more sound came and all that had distracted us from the heat and sun went away and the heat and sun flooded back in and I felt like I couldn't breathe. One more pop passed us and a black dot in the east, one last dot running, dropped and rolled. Shelly's eyes followed him to the ground. She looked back west, watched for movements, saw none.

—What happens now? Shelly said, still looking out over the valley.

—They take the vehicles that still work, I said. And any weapons lying around. Any ammo.

—And that's it?

—They fix the pumpjacks that were injured during the meeting.

—What else?

I tried to breathe, tried to pull in a full breath. I'd never struggled for breath before. I looked to see where Jake was but he was right where he'd been, beside me with Red.

—You okay? Shelly said.

—I'm fine, I said.

—What will they do with the bodies? Shelly asked.

—They'll take any bands they might want, I said.

—And then just leave them there?

—Yeah.

—Until the guys from the east come back to pick them up.

—Nobody will come back for the bodies, Shelly, I said.

She turned toward me with her eyes squinting, with lines on her forehead. Her eyes were intense, even through the scratches on her lenses. She was trying to understand something, or she had just begun to understand something. Something about bands and names and people and how these things were organized. Her head turned back to the valley with this new information. I wondered what the valley looked like now with this new knowledge, through those old scratched lenses. The lines on her forehead and the lines coming from the corners of her eyes stayed there.

—Are we heading to Cut Bank now? Shelly said.

I got in a full breath and my heart relaxed and I slowly let my air out.

—You okay? Shelly said.

—Fine, I said.

We all turned back in the direction of the truck and started walking. I heard Jake whisper to Red to follow us.

—We're heading to Cut Bank? Shelly said.

—That's right, I said.

—I thought no one lived in Cut Bank anymore.

—Not many.

—Then who's there?

—Joan. A friend of your mom's, I said. Friend of your dad's.

—Why do you want to see her?

—You still want to find out who the skeleton is? I asked.

—Yeah, she said. I want to find out. Do you?

I was less sure now. I hadn't expected her to ask. Her scratched lenses focused in on me and she was making sure I was still on her side, that I hadn't given up, that I still thought the name of the girl was worth looking for. Everything I had lived through told me it wasn't; everything the Front had taught me made it clear the girl's name did not matter.

—What are you thinking? she said.

—I do, I said. I want to find out.

She nodded. She'd pushed back against this new information about her world, about the value of things. And she'd made sure I was still pushing with her.

—Joan knew my dad?

—Yep.

Shelly nodded her head, encouraged by this.

—Get Red some water when we get to the truck, I told her.

—Some of the sweetwater? she said.

—Yep.

—He'll love it, she said. Jake smiled and nodded. So after Joan we head home, Shelly said.

—We head home, I said.

16 —Smells like Conrad, Shelly said.

—Yeah, I said.

I let the truck roll slowly down the road into the valley. The dim shades of near-white that had been in the sky while we were on top of the butte were gone now, replaced by the browns and blacks billowing out of exploded cars and damaged pumpjacks. These dark colors layered themselves across the valley and we coasted down below them, first below all the different shades of brown, and then below the blacks. The sun still beat down on us, soaking into the dark particulates that floated above us and around us, superheating the air we breathed, leaving no chance to expel heat from our bodies. Sunlight passed through these dark layers, flickering on every dry and dead corner of the valley, radiating from one lifeless object to the other, causing us to squint through the glare coming off the fallow fields, this unceasing brightness, blasting through to where there should have been shadows but where none existed. These fields were something less than fallow. They were not in a stage of regeneration. These fields were dead. Nothing new would come from them next season. All the next seasons had been played out of them, and all the next seasons lay together on the ground around us and any future rains that happened to fall wouldn't be enough to infuse any sort of life back into them. I pulled down the visor to block the fractured light that came through the crack in the top of the windshield. Shelly found her hat by her feet and pulled its brim tightly over her brow. Jake, his eyes nearly shut, watched the first of the valley's pumpjacks pass us on the right. Red sat behind us on the bench of the extra cab, his fogged eyes wide open, taking in all the brightness they could, searching for any shadows out there that would lend some contrast to the whiteness, shadows that would help him create a picture out of the light that entered his eyes, but there weren't any, other than the black plumes of smoke rising quickly from the smoldering fires.

We moved out across the flat plain. Bodies were scattered on the ground, a bullet having found its way around or through someone's cover. Some of the wounded were being attended to, but most sat shocked and alone, staring at their arms or legs that weren't whole anymore, parts of them ripped away. Others, who had escaped injury, kneeled next to the static limbs of the horseheads, analyzing them, trying to mend the parts of their iron bodies that had broken during the meeting.

At the point of revision a man stopped us with a wave of a hand. Other men stood behind him by the outpost, talking amongst themselves, rifles slung over their backs. The man looked at our plates and I pulled across the speed bump and stopped the truck. He walked up to my side, looked in the cab, looked behind the seats at Red, and leaned back and looked into the bed of the truck. He lifted the top of the cooler and stared into it for a moment.

He put his hands on my door and looked at Shelly and Jake. His hands were oil stained, or it could have been blood caked with dust. A strip of fabric tied together his ring and pinky fingers, and these two fingers, wrapped into one, trembled slightly, with nervousness or maybe pain, although he didn't show any signs of either.

—You go band hunting? the man said, nodding back at the cooler in the bed of the truck.

—No band on this one, I said.

—Unlucky, he said.

I nodded.

The man walked to the bed of the truck and leaned over with his nonbandaged hand and opened the cooler and pushed it over so the bones fell from it. He watched them scatter across the metal ridges of the bed. He leaned with both elbows on the rail. He readjusted the brim of his baseball cap and then just leaned and looked a while more. He walked back to my window and laid his bandaged hand on the rearview mirror.

—Just bones, he said. Who cares about bones?

—We're taking them back to the family they belong to, I said.

He chuckled at this and said, Okay. Sweat dotted the front of the man's T-shirt. He was my age; he was tired. The pumpjacks that had survived the meeting screeched around us. The man looked out past our truck and watched their arms counterlever up and down.

—You going where? Cut Bank? he asked.

—Yeah. Cut Bank.

He pushed himself gently from the mirror and walked to the front of the truck and looked again at the license plate.

—All the way from Conrad, he said through the windshield.

—Yeah, I said.

—You're taking the kids up to Cut Bank with you, he said, more as a question than a statement of fact.

—They're going with me, yeah. We have to talk to someone up there.

—Oh yeah, about the bones, he said.

—That's right.

—Who cares about bones? he asked again. He put his shaking and bandaged hand on the sill of my window. He didn't seem to notice its shaking.

—You mind if we get going? I said. I was glad I was with Shelly looking for the name of this girl. I was proud. Being with Shelly meant I was not with this man, that I was somehow pushing against him. Finding the name of the girl was a nearly impossible task, but it was the right task.

He tapped the toe of his shoe on the asphalt of the highway. Someone called him from behind. A door in the outpost opened and a man stuck his head out. He had a phone to his ear; he made a waving motion with his hand, telling the man we were talking to to let us go. The man we were talking to took a look at my band and then at Jake's.

—You take care, he said. Might be a few still alive out that way, looking to get one more round off.

He tapped the door with his bandaged hand and stepped away from the truck and then turned to walk back to the outpost where the man with the phone had been. His shoe had a loose tread like Shelly's had and it flapped against his toe as he walked. He turned back toward us.

—Don't stop on your way, he said. All those bands out there are ours now. I nodded and shifted the truck to drive and we moved out to the other side of the point of revision, out to the side where the battle had been lost, where the dead bodies and their bands lay. There were more bodies on this side. Those who weren't dead yet would be soon, bleeding out under the sun. We passed them, lying on the side of the road, holding themselves, the sun waiting for them to expire so it could inflate them with its heat, make them big and round as balloons. A cool shade enveloped our truck and a chill went through my body. I looked up through the windshield to see if there were thunderclouds above us but it was only thicker plumes of black smoke, from one of the pumpjacks, spewing upward. We moved back into the sun and the black cloud passed behind us.

—How long to Cut Bank? Shelly said.

—An hour, I said.

Red sat up behind us as we picked up speed. The last vehicle lay on its side, burning, fifty yards to our left. A body smoldered in the driver's seat.

—That smells bad, Shelly said.

—You can smell that from here? I said to her.

—No. But I know what burning bodies smell like, she said.

—Yeah, I said.

Jake nodded his head.

17 We left the black clouds of the burning cars and we headed north to Cut Bank. The oil wells moved along the valley next to us, plodding over the plains like Shelly's imagined bison, slowly trotting to the north in search of their sweetwater. The heat moved with us too. The sun, lower now, slanted in underneath the roof of the cab and through the broken glass of the windshield and it burned my arm, which rested on the sill of the open window. And it did smell like home, back in Conrad, just like Shelly had said. The air coming through the cab had a taste. I tried to remember the smell of the pine trees we'd sat under up by the spring, but the sulfur from the gas flares was just too strong, it didn't let my memory work, it made my nose burn. My eyes watered. My breath shortened.

—Why didn't they scan our bands? Shelly said.

—I don't know. Maybe the system was knocked out during the meeting.

Shelly pulled her watch from the chest pocket of her dress.

—What time is it? I asked.

—Seven thirty. She dropped the watch back into her pocket.

—Why'd that man seem more interested in your and Jake's bands than mine?

—What do you mean? I said.

She didn't answer.

—It's hot out, I said.

Shelly looked out east, away from the glare of the sun. She smoothed the wrinkles out of her dress.

—You need some water? I asked.

She pulled her cap down over her eyes so I couldn't see them, so she couldn't see me.

—What do you mean about the bands? I said.

She turned back to me.

—He kept looking at your band and Jake's band.

—Did he?

—You know he did.

—I don't know, I said.

—You do know.

—It's not important.

—That's a lie.

Jake was looking up at me now. Both of them stared straight through the sunlight coming through the window. The brightness didn't bother them now.

—It's not a lie, I said.

—Close enough.

—We can't do anything about it.

—So it's not important? she said.

—Exactly. We don't worry about the things we can't do anything about. Your mom taught you that. She taught me that.

—Because worrying about those things gets you in trouble, she said.

—That's it. It distracts from what's important.

—So what's important? Shelly said.

—Not the color of the band.

—But what is important? she asked. Her voice was rough now, the sulfur of the flares getting to it.

—Finding out who this girl is, I said.

—Those guys don't seem to think she's too important anymore.

—They're wrong.

—How could one thing be important to us and not important to someone else, she said.

—People are different.

—That doesn't seem right. Seems like if something is important it should just be important.

—That'd be nice, I said.

—Like a light bulb. On or off.

—Good analogy, I said.

—Don't make fun of me.

—I wish it were like that. I wish there were good and bad and that was that and everybody knew what was what.

She turned to look out east again, tracking oil wells as they went by.

—I'm not making fun of you, I said.

It was a half hour till sundown. No cool air came down from the mountains though. It was possible that there was no more cool air left, that it would never come, that the upper altitudes had simply run out of it. The shadow of the mountains was visible though. Its shade was nearing. Nearing slowly, but nearing. Sweat dotted the back of Shelly's neck. Jake's brow had beads on it too. I took my arm from the windowsill and put it in the shade of the door. It had burned enough for today.

—Why is the girl so important to us? Shelly asked.

I pushed the accelerator. We needed to get to Cut Bank before sundown.

—She just seems like a distraction, she said. I still couldn't see Shelly's eyes.

—She's not just a distraction.

—Seems like it. Maybe she's not important.

—Don't talk about her like that, I said. You wanted to find her. I agreed. I think you're right. You said you were in this with me. That there were two of us, not just one.

Shelly's eyes were watering. She blinked and a line of tears was taken by the wind past her ear and rolled down her neck.

—What happened to my dad? she said.

—What?

She didn't say anything.

—Shelly.

—It's not important? she said.

—No. Yes, it's very important.

—Important enough not to ever tell me anything about him? She coughed into the crook of her elbow. More tears came down her face. She wasn't crying though. Or if she was there was no sobbing. Just tears. Tears from the wind, from the glare through the cracks in the windshield, from one of a million specks of dust that had gotten into her eyes. I didn't know from what. From wanting to know what had happened to her dad.

—Shelly, I said.

—Don't say my name like that.

—I'm sorry.

—I'm not a little kid, she said.

—I know.

—Why is my dad so important that we can't even talk about him. She said this more as a statement than a question, as she often did with subjects she knew were important.

—He's the reason we're here, I said.

—Here where?

—Here alive.

She gathered the loose ends of her hair into the palm of one of her hands and held them together.

—Alive here how?

—We got out because of him. Got out of the war, the fighting.

Her hand tugged her hair down over her chest and then she let her hand hang there, clenching the locks together.

—They killed him and then let us out, she said. Her voice was calm, soft. I had to struggle to hear her over the wind coming through the window.

—Shelly, I said. Your dad, and then she softly interrupted me.

—Don't *Shelly* me, she said, reminding me she'd already warned me about this, but knowing all this hurt me too, her voice letting me down gently but firmly.

—I'm sorry, I said.

—It's okay.

—It's not okay.

—It's closer to okay, she said. Now that I know a little about it.

I nodded. Maybe. She let her black hair go and fiddled with her yellow band.

—He was blue? she said.

I nodded.

Shelly coughed again.

—Cover your mouth, I said.

—Sorry.

—It's okay.

Another line of tears came down her face. She wiped them away and looked straight into the wind coming through her window, squinting into it, more tears being pushed out of her eyes and over her cheekbone and toward her ear.

—I wish we could roll up the windows, Shelly said.

—Me too.

She turned around and looked over the seat at Red, lying down behind us on the small bench. She reached over to pet him. Jake turned around too.

—How much of all this have you known? I asked her.

She didn't answer; she said something to Jake about Red and Jake nodded his head.

—How long have you known it? I asked her.

She turned around and sat back down. She didn't say anything.

—How's Red doing? I asked.

—He looks good, she said. Tired but good. Probably a little thirsty.

—Yeah, I said.

Jake turned back around and sat in his seat too. Shelly adjusted her cap so it kept some of the low-lying sun from hitting her in the eyes. Jake sat on his hands again and squinted through the dusty glare of the sunlight coming through the cracked, dirty windshield.

—It's different when you tell me and I don't just hear it, she said.
She was such a good kid.
—I'm sorry, Shelly.
—It's okay.
—I'm sorry, I said again.

18   We pulled into the south side of town. Cut Bank had grown, and then it had collapsed. There had been jobs, but then those jobs weren't needed anymore. There was still oil, still gas, but the machines ran themselves. One person could service a hundred wells. The few remaining jobs to be filled had special requirements, a set of skills meant to protect the oil wells and their product, skills that were narrowly focused on how well you could eliminate those with intentions of competing for this product, skills that produced scenes like the one through which we'd just driven. If you were in it, if you were on a side, these were the jobs that were available.

—Where are we going here? Shelly asked.

I turned into a large parking lot and put the truck in the shade of a run-down building.

—What's this? Shelly said.

—I think this is the grocery store, I said.

—You've never been?

—No.

Back toward the street, remnants of a sign stood. Only its metal frame remained. What the sign had advertised had long ago fallen away, along with any light bulbs that had illuminated it.

—Is it open? she asked.

I turned the engine off.

—No. I don't think so.

—The shade feels good, she said. Her eyes closed and she rested her head against the seat.

—Any messages on the phone? I asked her.

She opened her eyes and I felt bad for taking her out of her small moment of relaxation in the shade of the grocery store.

—Where did I put it? she said. She tapped the pocket on her chest, the one with the watch in it, then she leaned over and ran her hand through the pocket on the passenger-side door.

—In your backpack, I said.

—Oh yeah.

She pulled the backpack up from underneath Jake's feet and opened a small outside pocket.

—Here it is.

—Any messages?

—Just one, she said.

—What?

Shelly flipped the phone open and pressed a button to open the message.

—It says, "Keep going."

—What else? Keep going what? Where?

—That's all it says.

—Give me the phone, I said, and she handed it to me.

I looked through the messages, searching for a missed one. All of them had been opened before. All of them read. I opened the most recent. "Keep going." I typed a message back and pressed send.

—What did you write? Shelly asked.

I pulled the lever for the hood. I gave the phone back to her and got out of the truck. She found the sent messages and opened the last one.

—"Where?" You don't know where to keep going? she said to me through the windshield.

I opened the hood and propped it up. Shelly and I couldn't see each other anymore. I heard her open her door and slide out and land on the asphalt of the parking lot. She walked around to the front of the car.

—Where are we going to go? Shelly said.

—Not sure.

—Where does Mom want us to go?

—North, probably.

—But we can't, Shelly said.

—I know that. I pulled the distributor cap from the engine and brought the hood back down. Get your backpack, I told her.

Jake was out of the car and handed the backpack to her.

—Thanks, she said to him.

—Leave Red. We won't be here long. He'll be fine with the windows down. Let's go, I said to them.

—Why would Mom say to keep going north if she knows we can't? Shelly asked.

I handed her the cap and she put it in her backpack. They walked close behind me toward the side of the building. I stopped at a metal door with no handle.

—There's no handle, Shelly said. Why would she say that?

—I know. I don't know. I knocked. Shelly started walking to the far end of the building.

—Where you going? I said. Stay here.

—I'm just checking. She got to the corner of the building and stood still. She didn't look back, didn't move.

—What's there? I said to her.

—A woman, she said.

—What?

She stayed still, not moving her gaze.

—She says to come here, Shelly said.

—Shelly, you wait. You don't go to her.

I got to her and pulled her to me and she stumbled backward but kept her footing. A woman sat on the bumper of a car in the last of the sunlight that came over the mountains to the west. She smoked a cigarette. Her shadow fell over her face and down in front of her and up against the unpainted cinderblock wall of the grocery store. It was Joan.

—Hey, I said.

—Hey. She flicked her cigarette to the ground and it smoldered there in her shadow.

—My sister tell you we were coming?

—No. Her aunt did, she said. Her hand was resting on her thigh. She lifted a finger to point at Shelly.

Jake came around the corner.

—She didn't say anything about him, Joan said, moving the finger to Jake. Joan looked at his band.

—Wait, whose aunt? Shelly said.

—Quiet, Shelly, I said.

—She said you had some bones, Joan said.

—Yeah, I said.

—Whose aunt? Shelly said again.

—Shelly, please, I said.

—You should throw those bones in the field over there and help your niece. Your niece and the boy. The boy and his band.

—My niece is fine.

—That's not what Jen said.

—Help isn't something we have access to.

—There must be some help somewhere, Joan said.

—Is Jen my aunt? Shelly said.

—There's nowhere, I said to Joan.

Joan stood up from the hood of the car. She stepped on her cigarette butt but it had already gone out.

—What do you know about the bones, she said.

—Girl. Twelve, thirteen.

—That's all you're going to know, Joan said. Just dump them. She served her purpose. Her family doesn't want to know any more about her either.

—You don't know that.

—I do. You need to go, Joan said.

—Where do we go? I said.

—Who's the boy? she said.

—Jake. We found him on the road. During the storm.

—You don't talk? Joan said to Jake.

—He's getting there, I said.

—Probably easier for you in the long run if he doesn't talk, she said to me.

—Stop that, I said.

—They try to take your band, Jake? she asked. Is that what they were after? You must be pretty fast. Pretty smart, too.

I shook my head at her, asking her to go somewhere else with her questions. She shrugged her shoulders.

—You know what happened to the girl, Joan said. You know why she was turned into bones on the bottom of the reservoir. You know why her family didn't go looking for her. But still you spend a day running around in this heat with your sick niece looking for answers that don't exist, and if there are answers that exist you already know them, enough of them anyway, but you're too dumb to acknowledge them.

—We're just looking for a name, I said.

—Her name doesn't exist anymore.

—Somebody knows it.

—It's been forgotten. Easier that way. You guys did the same thing. Joan looped her thumb through the belt of her jeans. She pointed it at Shelly again. She doesn't even know who her aunt is, Joan said, and let her finger drop.

—Is Jen my aunt? Shelly said.

—It's easy until it's not, I guess, Joan said. For the family of the girl, it's still easy. Or easier. Until you go digging in the reservoir and unearth everything they tried to bury. Joan kept looking at Jake, glancing at his band, looking back at me. She'd lit another cigarette and was talking again, her hands fast and smooth.

—You can get across now, she said. You should go.

—I can't do that.

—It's all a matter of limits. Once we pass all the limitations that we thought were in front of us, then our options are endless. Confronting those limits is the hard part. She took another deep long drag from her cigarette. She nodded, agreeing with what she had just said. Jake rotated his blue band around his wrist. He looked away from Joan and out farther, behind the grocery store, over a field of dry weeds and an old horse track and out farther still to the dry foothills that blurred into the glare of the sun. He closed his eyes from the glare and looked back to the front of the store.

—You have the same as mine, Joan said to Shelly.

Shelly looked at Joan's wrist as she shook it, the band not shaking much, tight around her skin, then she cupped a flame to her cigarette, which had gone out. She relit it and let the cloud of smoke sit there, in front of her face, without pushing it away.

—Yellow, Joan said to Shelly.

—I like yellow, Shelly said.

—Well, that's great, Joan said. Yellow dress, yellow band. That's nice.

—I know, Shelly said. She leaned against my hip, shading herself from the sun. She didn't like Joan too much.

—Well, at least she knows that, Joan said to me. She waved away the smoke that still hung in front of her face and sat back on the hood of her car.

Shelly pushed away from my leg and started coughing. She bent over and the waves ratcheted through her core. Her hands went to her stomach and she folded over, one knee touching the ground, her backpack running up on her shoulders. A spot of blood darkened the asphalt; a dark, thick, shiny film hung from her mouth. She let it hang there. I bent to her and wiped her mouth with my hand and rubbed my hand on the leg of my jeans.

—Jesus, Joan said. Shelly is who you need to be concerned about.

The quaking of her body stopped and she began breathing again, slowly and shallowly, her bunched hair falling past her cheek. I pulled it away. I put my hand on her back, under her backpack. I could feel the cracking of her lungs as she pulled and pushed air through them. She pushed off her knee and stood. Joan looked her over.

—You're a tough girl, she said.

Shelly nodded her head. Her eyes were closed.

—Hey, I said to her softly. Can you go to the truck? Get some sweetwater? Windows are open. Just reach in and pull the lock up.

Shelly nodded again. She opened her eyes. Her forehead was dotted with perspiration. It was cold to the touch.

—Can you take her? I asked Jake.

He nodded. He took her hand. They turned and walked toward the front of the store.

—You have any medicine? I asked Joan quietly.

She shook her head.

—We got a text from my sister. She said we can't go back to Conrad.

—I know, Joan said.

—What's happening down there?

—There've been some deals broken. Things are reshuffling. It won't be safe for a long time.

—So people without a side, I started to say.

—People without a side are game, she said. She flicked her cigarette away and it tumbled to the asphalt where the other one lay. New leaders. New laws, she said. The only laws that don't change are the ones of the bands. Colors don't change. You know all this. Blues are the favored ones. All the rest have their problems, restrictions. The bands are the one constant. Jake knows that. Almost as well as that girl whose name you're chasing.

Shelly yelled to me from the corner of the building.

—Wait, I told her.

—You need to get Shelly help. Forget about the name of the fucking bones.

Shelly yelled again.

—Baby, wait a minute, I yelled back.

—There's no list of names? I said to Joan. Aren't you still making all the lists?

—There's a man, Shelly yelled.

—What? I said. Shelly, you get over here. Jake! I left Joan and ran toward the corner. The two of them didn't move; they stayed at the corner, watching something, not taking their eyes from it. I pulled Shelly and Jake back behind me and saw the man Shelly had yelled about. He had the hood of the truck open and was digging at the spark plugs. He saw me and stuffed his wrench in his pocket and started running. He was a fat man. I watched him run. He got across the parking lot before he had to stop for breath. He'd need to stop for more. He tried to get going again, walking a few steps, trying to jump back to a run. He couldn't, so he walked, glancing over his shoulder as I followed him.

—Stay here, I said to Shelly and Jake over my shoulder.

The fat man tossed something from his pocket onto the ground. He stumbled over the discarded blocks of broken concrete that littered the field bordering the grocery store, refuse from a building that had been there years before and had been scrapped bit by bit. I picked up a stray piece of rebar that had a chunk of concrete still hanging on the end. The fat man threw another something on the ground. I found the first something he'd thrown: a spark plug. I picked it up.

—Drop all of them, I yelled to him, gaining on him.

He shuffled through the knapweed and thistle.

I was a handful of steps behind him now. He kept moving across the field, trying to run. His T-shirt was soaked through with sweat. I swung the ragged ball of concrete up behind my head and brought it around and into the side of his knee. He screamed a short, suffocated scream and buckled and tumbled to the ground, rolling onto a patch of thorns. He put his arms up over his head, his red band tight on his wrist. He blocked his head from me and my ball of concrete. I brought the rock of concrete down next to his head. Dust thudded up from the ground and drifted over the man's face. He didn't make a sound except for the air squeaking up and down his restricted throat, the weight of his chest suffocating him. Shelly nudged my thigh.

—What are you doing here? I said to her.

—Here are the rest of the plugs, she said and handed them up to me. Two from her and the one I had made three. I put them in my pocket.

—That everything? I asked the man as he suffocated under his own mass.

He nodded. Shelly stood by my side, watching the man suck breaths in and out.

—If my truck doesn't start. If there are some belts missing and it won't turn. I'm going to walk back out here and beat you some more.

He was crying now. Shelly kept watching him.

—You hear me? I said.

He cried more, not louder, just with thicker and quicker convulsions.

—Roll over on your side before you run out of air.

He rolled away from the thorns and away from the sun. His own shade darkened his face.

—You hear me? I said.

His breathing eased.

—Yes, he said, still sucking in air, trying to settle his lungs, still crying.

I turned and Jake was behind Shelly.

—What are you two doing here?

We walked back through the knapweed and thickets and past more broken blocks of concrete and more rusted rebar. The man lying behind us in the weeds hacked through a few breaths and stopped crying and then I couldn't hear any more from him. Joan was leaning against the bumper of our truck, looking at the engine. She had another cigarette going. I threw the lump of concrete and rebar into the bed. It clanged around and Shelly jumped at the sudden noise and I told her I was sorry. Red sat up and looked through the cab window.

—Why'd you have to go so hard on Chad? Joan said.

—Chad'll be fine.

—Lying out there suffocating himself to death, she said.

I turned and looked out where he lay and he rolled gently back and forth on his side.

—Chad'll be fine, I said again.

The kids climbed in the truck. I pulled the plugs from my pocket and found a wrench in the glove box. Shelly opened her backpack and handed me the distributor cap.

—Thanks, I said. She stayed quiet.

I walked to the front of the truck and waited for Joan to move and then started turning the plugs back into their spots.

—You know where the elementary school is? Joan asked.

—No, I said.

—Go there, she said.

—Where is it?

—Go into town. On your right.

—What's there?

—They might have something for Shelly.

I looked up from the engine, finishing the last twists of a plug.

—It's not a school anymore, Joan said. They treat people who don't have a side. Go there. It might not be there after tonight.

—Okay.

—And then get going, she said.

—Where? I said.

—You know what to do. She nodded at the cab where the kids waited for me.

—And if I don't want to do that?

—We all have our limitations. You have a few more than most people. That's nice. But we all cross them. However many we have. Wherever they are. One by one. She had her thumb through the loop of her jeans again. Again she raised her finger and pointed to where Chad lay, still rocking himself back and forth on his side, catching his breath.

—You should forget about those bones, she said.

—I heard you before.

—They won't bring anybody anything but trouble.

The last plug spun tight. The cap snapped on and I screwed it into place.

—What if I don't want to forget about the bones? I said. Don't you get tired of forgetting? I reattached the ignition wires to the plugs.

She flicked another cigarette butt to the ground. Smoke seeped out of her mouth. A breeze took it sideways across her face and then the smoke stopped coming out and I couldn't see the breeze anymore.

—The moment you think you need to remember is the moment you die, she said. Easier not to remember.

—Watch your fingers, I said to her and she pushed herself away from the truck. The hood fell shut and I wiped my hands on my pants.

—That meeting isn't over, Joan said. They're regrouping. It's moving up here.

With the hood down I could see the field again. Chad was up and limping away.

—Where was he trying to get? I asked.

—Away from here.

—Unlucky, I said.

—Last bit of luck left the Front a long time ago.

—Maybe we dug some back up out at the reservoir, I said.

—I don't think that's the type of luck you're looking for.

—I don't pick and choose the type of luck I find.

—You might want to, she said. She pulled the soft pack of cigarettes out of her back pocket and tried to shake one out, but none came.

—How much time you think I have before the meeting gets up here? I climbed in the truck. Red followed the sounds I made with his fogged-over eyes.

—I'd give it an hour.

—Perfect, I said.

I adjusted the rearview mirror and Red was there again with his pasty eyes locked on me. Behind him was the field and I couldn't see Chad anywhere. I turned my head out the window and the field was empty. I looked from edge to edge but couldn't see him. I turned back around and turned the ignition. The truck started up. I waited for Joan to push herself off the fender she was leaning on.

—We have an hour then? I said.

—Sure, Joan said. I can do that. She turned and walked slowly back around the corner. The last of the light from over the mountains lit her face and then she was gone.

—What happens after an hour? Shelly said.

—Did you get some of that sweetwater yet? I asked.

—Yeah. Both of us. You want some?

—That's good, I said. No thanks. We'll save it for later. You give any to Red?

—Yeah, she said.

—Good.

Shelly looked back at where Chad had been. I pulled out of the parking lot and Shelly turned to continue facing the empty field.

—He'll be fine, Shelly, I said to her.

—You sure?

—Sure, I said.

—Sometimes I think you're not very nice.

—Sometimes I think the same thing, I said.

—How do you do that stuff?

—What stuff?

—Hurt people. She stopped watching the field and turned around in her seat and slid to her butt. I shook my head, maybe to shake off her question. I didn't mean to shake my head. I didn't mean to ignore her question. Shelly kept looking at me.

—They'll be okay, I said.

—But you hurt them.

—That's right.

—But you didn't want to?

—I did, I said. I did want to hurt them.

—Is that okay? she asked.

—No. It's not okay.

—But kind of okay? she said.

—I guess, I said. No, I started again. No, it's not okay.

We drove with our shadow falling long in front of us, the sun bright in the rearview mirror and then gone, and our shadow gone too, and then just the rest of Cut Bank ahead.

—Are you okay with that? I asked.

—No, she said. I'm not okay with that.

—That's good.

She nodded, but she still wanted more. I was glad she wanted more.

—We left the side we were on so I wouldn't have to do things like that anymore, I said, trying to answer her question. Things really aren't better for us without a side. But I don't have to do things like that anymore. Like any of the things I've done today. Or at least not as often. And that's good.

Shelly looked ahead, thinking.

—Yeah. That's good, she said.

—I think so, I said, trying to determine if I really thought that. I thought I did.

—You okay? she asked me again, like she'd asked me outside the bar where we'd gotten the bottle of water.

—I don't know, I said. I don't think so. I'm sorry.

—It's okay, she said.

—Yeah.

She looked at me and I kept my eyes forward on the approaching town.

—What happens after an hour? she asked.

—It gets dark and Joan stops covering for us.

—She's on a side?

—Yeah.

—She's doing a favor for us?

—That's right.

—And then the favor stops.

—The favor stops then, yeah.

19   The streets of Cut Bank were empty. The stoplights swung in the wind, which had picked up. The lights were all out. I paused at each intersection but no other cars ever approached. I asked Shelly what time it was. She pulled her watch face out of her chest pocket.

—Eight thirty, she said.

—How's your throat?

—It's my lungs.

—How're your lungs?

She shrugged. They burn, she said.

—You should get another drink.

—I'm okay, she said. Save it for later.

—Okay.

—They have bison in town here, she said, looking at the oiljacks in people's yards and down the alleyways we passed. I nodded. Gas flares burned above the roofs of the houses, their colors more pronounced now with the sun behind the mountains, the orange waves fronting the purple sky now, more beautiful. The flames pushed shadows side to side behind the wireless telephone poles; they gave color to the cinder-block homes we passed. Shelly asked where the people were.

—In their houses, I said. Or gone already.

—Look at that, she said.

Up on the right an old man in his rocking chair sat on his front porch. He lifted his chin at us as we rolled by. I lifted a finger from the steering wheel. He looked back up the street behind us. The orange of flares rolled over the concrete of his porch steps.

—Who's he? Shelly said.

—Don't know, I said.

The man kept looking behind us, back in the direction of the meeting. Shelly looked behind us. A small radio sat on his porch rail. I couldn't hear if anything came out of it. I turned ours on again and pressed the scan button and waited for a station to stop its numbers from spinning. We passed the old man and Shelly was on her knees now looking at him out the back window.

—We're going to a school? Shelly asked, still watching the old man in his rocking chair.

—Yeah, right up here. The radio began to make a second pass through the numbers and I shut it off.

—We're not going to stay long? she asked.

—Turn around, I said.

Shelly slid back down to her butt and faced forward.

—Less than an hour, I said.

—What's at the school?

—Maybe some medicine for you.

—Are there teachers there?

—Some maybe. They're not teachers anymore though.

—Like you?

—That's right.

—Will they care about the bones? Shelly asked.

—They might, I said.

—That's good, right?

—Yeah, that's good.

—So there's medicine at the school? Shelly asked.

—There might be. They treat people there.

—They might have some extra, she said.

—They might, yeah.

She coughed.

—That'd be good, she said.

—Yeah.

I floated past the tattered stop signs of the neighborhood, looking left and right before pulling through each deserted intersection.

—And they might know her name, Shelly said. She had the girl's skull out again. It sat between her and Jake. Shelly had her forearm resting on it.

—I'm not sure, Shelly. They might.

She took her watch out of her chest pocket and leaned forward into the light of the flares that came through the windshield.

—Forty-five minutes until we need to leave Cut Bank, Shelly said.

—Okay, I said. We won't be long.

20 Only three cars occupied the parking lot of the elementary school. A guard with a shotgun leaned against one of them. I parked the truck a few spaces down from where he stood. He lifted his head from his phone and watched us get out.

—Leave Red, I told Jake.

—Okay, Jake said.

—Do we need to take stuff out of the engine? Shelly asked.

—We're going in for a minute, I said to the guard.

—Your truck's fine, the guard said.

—We'll just be a little bit.

He put his head back down to his phone, not acknowledging what I'd said, or maybe not hearing. He closed his phone and put it in his pocket and readjusted the strap that held his shotgun across his back. He looked back up at us.

—Yeah, it'll be fine, he said to me.

—Thanks, I said.

We entered the school's front doors. We walked down the main hallway. Its walls were hung with assignments, drawings, posters. A calendar from June was stapled to the wall outside a classroom. A party hat was pinned to June 12th. The calendar was four years old. At the end of the hall, we found the administrative offices. Manila folders of tardy slips and unexcused absence sheets hung from the main door. A table next to the door had messy piles of half sheets describing various illnesses and how to treat them. Jake flipped through them and grabbed one that said something about coughing and lungs and blood. He gave it to Shelly. Shelly read through the bullet points.

—Do we have any of this stuff? she asked me, pointing at the medications in bold print.

—Grandpa might have that, I said, putting my finger on *aspirin*.

—That's it? she said.

—Yeah.

—Aspirin's for headaches, she said.

—Well, maybe you'll get a headache and then you can use it, I said.

—I hate headaches.

—Me too.

She put the slip back on the table.

Inside the door of the admin offices, a corkboard had pictures of schoolchildren pinned to it. The door was locked. I clicked the knob back and forth. A door squeaked open somewhere behind us, around a corner and down a hall.

—You hear that? Shelly asked.

—Yeah.

The three of us turned and listened.

—Did it come from that hallway, that one, or that one? Shelly asked, pointing at each.

Jake pointed to the one farthest to our left. The open door, around the corner and down the hall, let a few voices through, then it softly shut again and the voices stopped. Footsteps followed this silence. A woman came around the corner and approached us. She walked through the last glow of the twilight shining through a window from the west, dull and soft, and passed back into the darkness of the hallway between us and her. She passed by one more window and the western glow caught her long hair, hair like Shelly's, hair like my sister's, long and dark, and then she disappeared again until she was with us under the dim fluorescence of the solitary light that hung from the ceiling.

—Can I help you? she asked us, looking at me first, and then at the little ones, a soft smile matching the soft sound of her voice.

I pointed at the offices.

—It's locked, she said.

—I know.

—Can I help you? she asked again kindly.

—Those pictures. The kids.

—Do you want to see them? she asked.

—Yeah. Please.

She pulled a ring of keys from her pocket and it jingled and filled the hallways with its sounds of small metal on small metal. She stepped gently past us, placing her hand on Shelly's head and letting it slide off slowly as she moved to the door. She unlocked the door and welcomed us through, smiling at Shelly and Jake again as they walked past her. They both smiled up at her. She flipped a bank of light switches until she found one that worked. Greenish white light fell from the ceiling.

The pictures were behind a secretary's desk. They were grouped in years. Boys and girls together.

—They were disappeared? I said. I couldn't see any of their faces clearly, the greenish light didn't reach this side of the room. I moved closer, leaning over the desk toward the children.

—Yes, she said.

—Did they find any?

—Yeah, she said.

—Where'd they find them?

—What do you mean? the woman asked me.

—How did the families find them? I asked.

—You mean find them alive? Where did they find them alive? she said. Her voice was calm and quiet and hollow. Her voice moved through the small office as if it were the only sound moving through the universe, the only waves pushing and vibrating across an enormous void between her and me. Her voice was clear and delicate and sturdy, and I would have missed it had I not been listening for it, had I not been ready for each word.

—Yeah, I said. How'd they get them back to their families?

—They're never found alive, she said. She looked at me as though I must not be from the Front. I could hear the buzzing of the fluorescent bulb across the room now. I could hear the bottoms of Shelly's red tennis shoes twisting slightly on the thin carpet of the office. The woman continued speaking.

—They're found in ditches. In the oilfields. In alleyways. Not all of them are found. Some stay disappeared. But they never reappear alive.

—We found one, Shelly said.

—Oh really? the woman said, her voice still calm and caring and interested.

Shelly nodded.

—Where? the woman asked.

—In the reservoir.

The woman stayed quiet, but stayed understanding.

—It was a skeleton, Shelly said.

—Some are, yeah, she said.

—I have her skull in my backpack.

—Shelly, can you and Jake go into the hall, please? I said, wishing my voice sounded soft but sturdy like hers.

Neither of them moved. Like me, they kept staring at the pictures of boys and girls pinned to the corkboard. There were dozens of children. More each year, the most recent year's children pinned at angles, hanging at the edges, some overlapping others.

—Just right outside the door, I said.

—Okay, Shelly said.

Jake turned and Shelly followed him. She pulled the door gently closed behind her.

—Sweet kids, the woman said.

—Are the disappeared ever found with bands on? I asked her.

—No.

—They're all blue?

She nodded and said yes.

—Why is it happening so often now? I said.

—It's always happened. Ever since the first person was banded.

—Not like this though. Not like this.

—How old was your skeleton?

—Not older than thirteen, I said.

—How long had she been in the reservoir, she asked.

—Maybe four years.

The woman stepped behind the desk. She pointed at the last group of photos.

—These children were all disappeared four years ago.

—And how about the ones after that?

—The school closed. We stopped keeping track, she said.

I moved behind the desk to look more closely at the children. I tilted the photos left and right, revealing and hiding faces. The pin in one picture popped out and the photograph fell to the floor. I picked it up and turned it over. Terry Rose. I pinned her back with the others of her year.

—Are you the principal here? I said.

—Was.

—You're a teacher? she asked.

—Was, I said.

—Not many people bother tracking down the disappeared, she said.

—Did they find Terry Rose? I asked.

The principal shook her head. The room was quiet. The principal stood still. We looked at Terry on the corkboard, surrounded by her disappeared classmates.

Shelly knocked on the window of the office door. She showed me her watch. She flashed five fingers at me four times. Twenty minutes. She went back and sat with Jake, their backs leaning against a wall.

—Sweet kids, the principal said again. She pushed her band up and down her wrist, spinning it, turning it, pushing it up against the pad of her thumb and then letting it slacken again. We all had our own habits we'd formed with our bands. These movements were part of who we were. The rest of her body was calm, though, not at ease, not resigned, but not nervous, not anxious about the approaching meeting. She was living as each of us lived, weathering the storm, the storm not yet over, not knowing what life would be like without the storm. We had been born into it, it was the only thing we'd known. More and more of the anchors to something different—a time before the storm—died each year. Old people now questioned their own connections to the time before the storm, questioning away that other world of theirs, doubting it, like some memory they no longer had any confidence in, because that memory was just too different now, was just too far away from what this storm was, and how big this storm was. We were all in it, and none of us believed any of us would make it to a time where there wasn't a storm.

—They're sweet kids, yeah, I said. We looked at them through the window as we had looked at the kids pinned to the corkboard.

—This isn't going to be any normal meeting, she said. She spun her band once more and dropped her arms to her sides. Her band was green.

—What do you have? I asked, pointing quickly to her band.

—They say a bad heart, she said.

She looked at my band, fitting tightly to my wrist, my wrist hanging tensely at my side. She smiled slightly and nodded, maybe happy for me, maybe not, maybe worried for me.

—Why do you stay? she asked.

—My family. Sister, my niece Shelly, parents.

—You the only blue? she asked.

—Yeah.

She nodded her understanding.

—You have family? I asked.

She nodded again, more hesitant now.

—A blue and a yellow. Girl and a boy. Twins.

—Were they at the school?

—Both. A while back. You met my son out front. I sent my girl across four years ago.

—Their dad?

—He's blue. He went with her.

—You don't hear from them then, I said.

—No. No communication. Helps assimilation, they say.

—So you don't know how they are.

She offered no nod or movement of her shoulders. No sign of having heard me. She just stared at me. Then her eyebrows narrowed a bit.

—You're a good boy, she said.

—I'm not that good, I said.

—Protecting others makes you do bad things. You should try to go easy on yourself. There are enough people that'll go hard on you.

—I'll try, I said.

She nodded. Her eyebrows relaxed.

—Shelly's yellow, she said. What does she have?

—Small lungs. Underdeveloped. Compressed by her sternum. Always infected. She needs medicine, I said.

—I wish I had something for her.

—No medicine here?

—No. We've been out for a while now. We just patch things up here. Nothing much gets healed.

Jake and Shelly were smiling about something. Jake said something to Shelly and she laughed and said something back. Jake nodded his head and smiled.

—He hasn't really talked all day, I said.

—Is he your niece's friend?

—Classmate. Friend now.

—She knows people. Knows what people need, the principal said.

—Yeah. She's a builder. She can't stand dissonance. I think she understands it, but she works against it when she sees it, when she hears it. She keeps us together.

—Did Jake find the skeleton with you?

—No. We picked him up in the windstorm today.

—What was he doing out in the storm? she asked.

—Running from something.

—The storm saved him. Then you saved him from the storm, she said.

—He's a strong kid. He would've been fine.

—He would have suffocated, she said.

The deep waves of a distant bomb bumped the windows and

thudded against the walls. Shelly and Jake stood up and looked at us through the office window, their smiles gone, their faces serious again.

—Meeting is starting, the principal said.

—Yeah.

Shelly brought her watch out and flashed me her hand three times. Fifteen minutes.

—You're a lot like your niece, she said to me.

—Sometimes, I said. I hope so. She's the best of us.

A small series of distant gunshots rolled through the room. Shelly opened the door.

—We have to go, she said to me.

—Yeah, we're going, I said.

—It was nice to meet you, the principal said to Shelly.

—It was nice to meet you too, Shelly said. She smiled at the principal and pulled the door further open for me to walk through.

—Thanks for your time, I said to the principal.

—Thanks for yours, she said.

—You'll stay here through the meeting? I asked her.

—Yeah.

—Will you be all right?

—I don't know, she said. Seems like new laws might form tonight. The spaces for people between sides get smaller with each meeting.

I nodded. We walked out the door. Shelly let it close behind us. The principal took her ring of keys from her pocket and locked it.

The glow of the twilight was gone. The only light came from the flat fluorescent bulb above us. We all looked pale and tired. Shelly's dress was more green than yellow. The shadows on our faces were depthless and out of focus.

—Bye, Shelly said.

—Bye, baby, the principal said. We walked down the hallway toward the parking lot. The vibrations of another bomb came through the hallway walls; the fluorescent bulb flickered. Shelly's legs, beneath her greenish yellow dress, sped up. She told me to hurry.

21 The principal's son leaned with his shotgun against our truck. The door closed behind us and he stood up straight and closed his phone. The pulse of gunfire passed us, floating among the houses of the surrounding neighborhood, still blocks away, perhaps still on the edge of town. The edges of the houses lit up with the muzzle flashes that framed them from behind, halos of light that outlined the roofs and telephone poles. The center of the meeting was in the west, like an electrical storm coming in over the mountains, and the four of us stood in the parking lot and watched the flashes as if it really were an electrical storm, wondering when the rain would reach us, or if everything would blow itself to the north and miss us. We waited for, almost hoping for, the big strike, the one that reached across the sky above us, the one that came out from under the clouds and showed itself, crooked and bright and gone before you could look at it as closely as you wanted to.

This was how these nighttime meetings started—a commotion that drew your eyes and ears toward it, your eyes and ears waiting and hoping for more, your eyes not able to break free from the light. The bright whites that hung in front of the clouds, which blinded you for a second and burnt in the crooked tree that stood across the street, the lightning rod standing crooked on top of the neighbor's house. Light that blinded you until, between strikes, you finally made yourself move to safety, or to somewhere safe enough so you could miss the rain for one more day.

—You going south? the principal's son asked.

—Was, I said.

—Where you going now? he asked.

—I don't know. I took my eyes from the light flashing around the houses. Another flash came through the neighborhood and his face appeared and then faded again.

—East, he said. Try east. I strained to see his face without the flashes of light. He wasn't old. He was younger than me. But he'd seen things. And I guess I had too. But they'd touched him differently. He was still good. His eyes were calm, kind. He'd still make the right choices.

—If you can make it through the night, you might be able to head south again, he said.

—Okay, I said.

—The best way to sit out the night is east. Find a side road. Watch which way the lights of the meeting go. Avoid them. Then in the morning, maybe south.

—Are there still more of us out there? I asked.

—There're a few. Not many. Don't count on finding them.

—Get in the truck, I told Shelly and Jake. I unlocked my door. Red stuck his nose out from the back bench. His tail thumped back and forth. The deep concussion waves made him nervous.

—Hey, Red, Jake said and patted him on the head. Red's ears went flat and he got a couple licks on Jake's arm.

The kids climbed in on my side and slid across the seat and I got in after them. I closed the door and rolled down the window. Jake made sure his door was locked.

—And if I can't get east? I asked the principal's son.

—You need to get east, he said. He nodded at me to get going.

I started the truck.

—Don't look for any of us out there, he said. There's not enough of us. Everyone has a side. You'll never find us.

—Okay, I said.

I pulled the truck out of the parking lot and headed away from the flashes in the west. They reflected off the passenger rearview and across

Jake's and Shelly's faces. It was dark in the east. I kept our headlights off, traveling by the light of the gas flares that came through the alleyways we passed. The reflections of the flares slid up over the hood of the truck and over the windshield. Some flared higher than others, their gases burning longer into the heights of the sky. There should have been stars. I looked up through the glares and the cracks in the windshield. There should have been. It was a clear night. No clouds. No moon. But I couldn't see any, couldn't remember when I'd last seen one. Jake and Shelly swayed left and right as I moved the truck around the potholes in the street. They were silent as I drove the truck out of town and out onto the dark, flat expanse that stretched eastward.

—It's pretty, Shelly said.

We were five miles east of town now, on a small hill perched above the plains. I pulled the truck onto a side road and continued a few hundred yards more. I brought it to a stop but left the engine running. A thousand flares revealed topography that otherwise would have been dark and unseeable.

—Yeah, I said. It is pretty.

—You used to have campfires, right? she said.

—When I was a kid?

She nodded. I looked west, checking on the meeting, checking to see if anyone had followed us.

—Yeah. I think so.

—And then you'd count the stars.

—I think so, yeah. That's right. There were stars, I said.

—Like the windshield stars. Until you couldn't anymore and then you'd fall asleep.

—That sounds right, yeah.

The flashes in the west were distant now, as if the meeting had moved westward, or been pushed north.

—Who told you about the stars? I asked.

—Mom.

—She'd know, I said.

—Why'd you stop the truck? Shelly asked.

—It might be safe here for a while, I said. If no one comes this way, we'll be safe for a bit.

—Until morning?

—I don't know, Shelly. I hope so.

—Me too. Then maybe Mom will call again and say things are okay back home.

—Yeah, I said. I hope so.

—Yeah.

—Did she tell you where we camped? I asked her.

—When you counted stars?

—Yeah.

—Little Rock something, she said, which was right.

—Little Rock Coulee.

—That's it. She smiled. Good memory.

—Thanks, I said. That's not too far from here.

The dull thud of a distant explosion passed us. The windshield vibrated. A small glow came and went in the rearview.

—What else did we do there? I asked her.

She looked at me, her eyes narrowed a bit, surprised I was asking her. I was the one who had been there. I was the one who had done these things.

—You fished there, Shelly continued. For Arctic grayling. Because that was your favorite fish. Although they were small. Shelly kept looking at me. I kept listening to her.

—That's right, I said.

—Not as big as the rainbows. And definitely not as big as the whitefish. But definitely more beautiful, she said.

—You're right.

—They had that thing on their backs.

—A dorsal fin. Big. From their neck to their tail. Beautiful.

—And they were rare, even then.

—Yeah.

—And they didn't stink. Not like the whitefish stank.

—No, they didn't stink. As she mentioned each detail, the memory came back to me, as if she was telling me about my childhood, the childhood I'd forgotten about, lost.

—They poked your hands, she said.

—Yep, the dorsal fins had points on them.

She nodded.

—I didn't tell you any of these stories, did I? I said to her, or asked her, I couldn't tell which.

—Grandma did. Mom some. But Grandma mostly. She told me what you guys did. And what you guys liked and didn't like.

—She liked brown trout, your mom, right?

—Bull trout, Shelly said. Farther upstream.

—That's right, I said.

I looked at her, but could only see her when flashes of light came off the mirrors, carrying the explosions that thudded behind us.

—Have you ever fished? I asked her.

—There aren't any fish in the reservoir, she said. No rivers.

—No, I said. There aren't.

—I'd like to someday, though, she said.

Another flash came off the mirrors, a little brighter, a little closer. Her face, in the brief light, seemed to know she'd never see these fish. But she continued talking.

—Tell us a childhood, she said.

—Tell you a childhood?

—Yeah.

Volleys of gunfire were audible again behind us. Dim, still, small pops between the explosions.

—We should go, I said. Down in the flames of the valley there was a small dirt road that would take us further east, where we could hide more safely, down in a gulley, a draw, somewhere with better cover.

—Wait, Shelly said. First a childhood. But it can't be of the reservoir. I've been there. It doesn't count.

—Okay, I said.

—Just a short one. It doesn't have to be long. One of you and Mom.

I tried to think of my sister and me out exploring by ourselves on the Front, walking through hills, down a creek, or farther up in the mountains. Each effort only brought back browns and grays. I couldn't tell if some of the stories were mine. I couldn't tell if I was in them. The color wasn't there. I didn't have any of my own memories.

—Just a short one, Shelly said again. The sounds of the meeting had dimmed again, their percussions muffled, the edges taken off.

—I don't remember one, Shelly, I said to her.

—Just one, she said.

—Shelly.

A brighter flash came from behind us and lit up her face. She was confused, perhaps matching my confusion. Another flash and she was frustrated, as if I were keeping a secret from her.

—I can't think of one, baby, I said.

She didn't believe me.

—Something from when you were a kid. Something like what we did today at the sweetwater.

—I don't remember, Shelly. She saw that I was looking her in the eyes, a little too directly, maybe, too intently, my words too harsh, too much of my frustration showing through.

Her chest was agitated now. She tried to breathe in and then let what air she had out in one smooth exhale. She was partially successful.

—How am I going to know then? she said when her breathing was calm again.

—Know what?

—What there was? she said quietly.

—I don't know, Shelly.

—Do you know what there was? she asked.

—I don't think so, Shelly. It's all gone.

I put the truck in Drive.

—How can you not know? she asked. She coughed and leaned her mouth into her elbow.

—When we get home we'll have Grandma tell us some childhoods, okay?

—You don't know any? she asked again.

—I don't know, I said.

—You think we'll get home?

—I don't know, I said. I didn't want to sound frustrated. I was though.

Flashes appeared in front of us now, a little to the right, back to the south, down in the valley of the flames. Another, smaller, meeting had started. The flashes were small but sharp and crisp and broke through the soft red haze of the flares. I let off the brake and the truck started rolling east, dropping into the flares below us.

—Is the south blocked? Shelly said.

—It is right now.

—What'll we do?

—We'll get down from this hill. Find a gulley. Stay out of sight until morning.

Shelly coughed again. Jake reached for a bottle of sweetwater and put it in her lap. A hole snapped through the back window of the cab. Shelly screamed and I pulled her toward me and I reached for Jake but he was already down. I took the truck off the road and into the field of pump-jacks and flares. I heard an engine rev up on the hill we'd just come off of, then another. Dead sage whipped past the truck. Another hole snapped through the back cab window. Shelly and Jake were tossed about on the seat. We made it to a dry creek and I followed it east until I reached a larger dry riverbed, still headed east. Shelly sat up and pushed Jake up with her.

—Stay down, baby, I said.

—I think Jake threw up, Shelly said.

I pulled behind a stand of dead cottonwoods. I cut the engine and listened for the trucks that had been behind us. There was one up on the ridge to the south. Its headlights made cones through the dust and haze hanging in the air. It didn't move. If there were still other trucks nearby, I couldn't see or hear them.

—Okay, I said to Jake. Let's see.

Jake didn't move.

—It's on my dress, Shelly said.

—Jake, I said.

—Look at my dress, Shelly said. A dark circle covered her stomach.

—Jake, Shelly said.

Shelly leaned over toward Jake, trying to see what was the matter with him. I pushed her against the back of the seat. I ran my hand over Jake's back. It was wet. The same darkness on Shelly's dress covered my hand.

—What is that? Shelly said.

—Shelly, hush. I pushed her away again but she kept leaning forward, trying to wake Jake. I tugged her away and pushed Jake against the seat back like I had Shelly. His chest was wet now. It was red in the light of the flares that came through the branches of the cottonwood. Shelly screamed again. I told her she had to be quiet. The truck up on the ridge shut its lights off. I pressed the holes in Jake's skinny rib cage together, one hand on his chest, the other on his back. He woke and let out a scream and struggled against my arms. His body tensed. A flash came from back up the creekbed. Shelly put her hands over mine.

—Ready? I said to her.

—Ready, she said. I slipped my hands out from under hers and she pressed the wounds together. Jake screamed again. The truck on the ridge turned its headlights back on.

I started the truck and tore out from behind the cottonwood and the oilrig and its flare and headed farther east, farther down the riverbed. White light flashed in our mirrors. The sandy riverbed opened and veered north. The bend in the river cut the flashes from view. I kept the truck moving fast through the sand and gravel, headlights still off, cutting through the shadows falling over us from both sides, their dark swaths rolling up and over the windshield. Shelly's hands slipped off of Jake and she repositioned them and pressed her hands together harder around his small body. Jake didn't move. Less sound came from him.

A bridge traversing the riverbed appeared up ahead. I told Shelly to hold on. I picked out a clearing on the left of the riverbank and took the truck into it, the truck bounced up the bank and revved higher, we broke through a barbed-wire fence and its barbs screeched over our hood and up our windshield. Shelly fell over Jake as his body leaned toward the door. She tried to pull him up into a sitting position. We came out onto a service road for an oilrig and I followed it to the road that led to the bridge. I turned in the opposite direction of the bridge and continued north. There was only the orange of the gas flares in our rearview mirrors. I couldn't see any headlights. Didn't see any more flashes. I kept the truck going for a mile more and then pulled over.

—What are you doing? Shelly asked.

—Let me see Jake.

Shelly kept her hands tightly around either side of his rib cage. Her hands were black with blood. I put my hand to Jake's neck and waited for a pulse. I shifted my hand and waited some more. I pressed harder into where his jugular should have been pulsing in my hand.

—I hear something, Shelly said.

I spun around and looked out the back of the cab.

—No, in here, she said.

—What?

—Quiet.

It was coming from her backpack.

—The phone, she said.

I let go of Jake's neck and scrambled through the backpack. I found the phone and looked at the screen.

—It's your mom, I said. I put one hand back on Jake's throat, his small Adam's apple, his slender neck; I searched for the pulse while I opened the phone but the phone slipped out of my hand, covered in blood. It thudded on the floor and I swept my hand back and forth to find it, dust and dirt sticking to my fingers. My hand knocked against it and I picked it up. My sister was already saying something.

—I'm here, I'm here, I said to her. I kept my finger looking for a pulse. I pressed deeper.

—Where are you? she said. I couldn't hear her well.

—What's going on there? I asked.

—Where are you? she said again.

—East of Cut Bank. We're waiting to get south tomorrow. We're looking for a place to stay until daybreak.

—Don't. Don't try. Go north.

—We'll wait, I said. Tomorrow we'll be able to get back south. I couldn't find any pulse in Jake's neck. I tried the other side.

—No. You won't.

I heard my dad yell something in the background.

—Go north, she said again. Get across.

—Across the Line? I said.

—Yes, she said.

—We'll get south, I said.

—Even if you could, we won't be here.

—What?

—Things are done here. They're forcing us out.

Our mom was talking in the background now.

—Put Mom on, I said. What's she saying?

—The agreement is off, my sister said.

—Jake's not moving, Shelly said.

—Quiet, Shelly, I said.

—Jake's not moving, she said again.

My hand was on both sides of Jake's neck now. My fingers soft but deep on either side of his trachea. Nothing.

—Where will you go? I asked my sister. So we know.

—We don't know, she said. Wherever we're forced.

My mom told her to tell me goodbye, to get off the phone.

—How's Shelly? my sister said.

—Shelly's going to be fine, I said.

—Get north, my sister said again. She was yelling.

—We will.

—Tell her I love her, my sister said.

—I will.

—Bye, she said. Her phone clicked shut.

I took my hand from Jake's neck. I wiped the blood onto the seat. The old dog whined. The oilrigs around us whined. Their flames washed red over the windshield.

22 I got out of the truck. I walked to the passenger side and opened the door. Jake slumped out toward me and I stopped him from falling out on the ground.

—Let go of him, I said to Shelly. She still had her hands around his chest, still pressing in. She shook her head and kept pressing. I pushed her away and put an arm under Jake's legs and the other across his back and lifted him out of the truck. His head fell so far back, so far back and away from his shoulders. I laid him on the asphalt of the highway. His bent knees fell to one side and his body rested there, twisted and bloody. I heard Red jump out of the truck. Shelly came and stood by my side. Blood covered the front of her yellow dress; a blank stare covered her face.

—Get Red back in the truck, I said.

—What are you doing, she said. Her voice was so sweet. My niece was so sweet. Her red shoes had red blood on them. She'd lost her red cap somewhere. Her black hair reflected red light from the fields of flares. Her black hair was tangled behind her ears; it fell tangled down her chest. She asked me again in her sweet voice what I was doing.

—Get in the truck, Sweetheart. Wait there. I'll be right there.

She didn't move. I stood and reached into the bed of the truck and found the ball of concrete with the rusted rebar protruding from it, the one I'd used to down the fat man walking as fast as he could away from me. I knelt down beside Jake and laid his right hand flat against the dark asphalt.

—Uncle, no, Shelly said.

—Quiet, I said.

—No, she said again, so sweetly.

The ragged ball of concrete was heavier than I remembered. I turned Jake's hand on its side; I held his forearm with my thumb across the smooth skin of its underside. I brought the ball of concrete above my shoulder. I only had to let it fall, it came down with such force. I brought the wretched piece of concrete down and heard Jake's little wrist splinter apart and become a loose bag of sharp pieces underneath its tight, smooth skin. Red jumped on me, biting at my hands. I threw him aside and into the ditch. The old dog was all bones under his ragged skin. Shelly cried and screamed. I let the ball of jagged concrete fall one more time. Jake's blue band slid off his shattered wrist easily. Shelly turned and ran. I dropped the band and ran after her, overtaking her quickly, her strides so small, and I took her to the ground.

—I like my yellow one! she screamed.

—You be quiet, I said through a tangle of her dark hair that covered my face. I dragged her by the arm through the dust on the side of the road. She stood and dug her red tennis shoes into the asphalt and pulled to get away. I pulled her back toward me and she fell and I dragged her to where Jake and the concrete ball lay. I threw her next to Jake and put her chest to the ground. I sat on her back. Her face was tight against the asphalt, a stream of tears pooled beneath her cheek, dust billowed up and onto her face, into her lungs. She hid her right arm underneath her body and I dug for it and yanked at it until it came free. She struck the side of my leg with her other fist. Red was on me again with his old, dull teeth and I threw him again into the ditch and he tumbled through the weeds and grasses there.

—You don't do that to Red, Shelly sobbed. You don't hurt Red!

—Quiet, I yelled.

I caught her whaling fist and pinned it under my knee. She got it loose and she started pummeling me with it. I ignored her blows. I let her have them. My weight pushed the air out of her lungs, and with no air to bring them voice, her screams fell away. I caught her right hand and tipped it on its side like I had Jake's. Her wrist fell apart with the first blow. The pain of it brought air back into her lungs. She lifted me up with her breath. But she only cried now. No screams. She held them in now. She only sobbed. I was the one screaming now. I couldn't stop. I pushed her yellow band, the yellow that matched her favorite yellow dress, up onto her wrist but it wouldn't slip off. I pushed harder and her sobs deepened and I screamed harder and the sobs vibrated through my body and shook the flares growing up into the sky around us. I lifted the broken block of concrete in the air and brought it down on her little wrist again. Bones ground apart beneath her skin. No screams from her. No big breath, either. Just sad cries, sad sobs. I caught my breath. I cried. I pushed the yellow band over her collapsed wrist and felt around for Jake's band. I found it lying in the dust and gravel beyond the rumble strips and cupped her fingers together with mine, pressing the tattered wrist as small as it would go, and pushed the band over her hand. I rolled off of her and her lungs brought in a long breath and she let out air in gasps and convulsions. She cried in a mess of tears and coughs and slowly brought her bending wrist close to her chest. Red was limping out of the ditch. He limped past me and went to Shelly and in sobs she apologized to him for what I had done. She told Red it was okay. She kept sobbing, telling him it was okay. He nudged the hair from her face with his nose. He licked the tears from her face.

—We need to go, I said.

I knelt beside her and threaded my hands and arms underneath her neck and knees and placed her broken wrist softly on her chest. I lifted her gently. I stepped up with one foot and then got the other foot under me and I stood. Red walked to Jake and sniffed his cheeks and neck and sniffed the blood that covered his chest. I carried Shelly to the open passenger-side door and gently set her down on the seat. I shut her door and stepped over Jake and over Red lying beside him and over the ragged concrete ball. I looked at Red to see if he was coming, but he was staying with Jake, his foggy eyes trained on Jake's face, ignoring me. I leaned into the bed of the truck and grabbed as many of the little girl's little bones as possible and threw them as far as I could into the night, not wanting to hear them land, not wanting to see them again. I kept grabbing them and throwing them until I couldn't reach any more and then I opened my door and felt around for the girl's skull and I found it and I turned to the badlands that stretched out into the darkness around us and I heaved the skull out to where the bones had scattered into the night, never to be found or cared for again. I got in the truck and we drove to the Line.

23   We stopped and a man walked to the side of the truck and shone a flashlight into the cab. He paused it on Shelly. She was in an old shirt and pair of jeans of mine. I had made her throw her yellow dress out the window as we drove. The clothes sagged off of her small body. The man shone it on her face and she stared back at the light without squinting, as if the light were not entering her eyes. The man shone it across my face and I shut my eyes until he moved it away. He stuck a scanner into the cab and I moved my band to it and it dinged and lit blue and he offered it to Shelly. She lifted her wrist slowly and the scanner and her wrist met and it dinged and lit blue. Shelly lowered her wrist back onto her lap. A tear came down her face. He pulled the scanner out of the cab and waved us through. I drove us over the Line.

Sunlight came from the east, slow and red and flat along the prairie, which stretched unbroken across the horizon. There were no other cars on the road and there was no break in the oilrigs that bordered the road and stood like bison in the prairie. We crested a hill and I pulled over to the side of the road. The flares on this side of the Line blended, in the east, with the sunrise, its colors now turned orange, but the darkness to the west kept the flares burning strong and bright and gave definition to the hills that began over there and to the mountains that sat farther still.

Shelly opened her eyes. She grimaced and shut them again. She cupped her hand tenderly to her stomach.

—Bison are over here too, she said softly, sadly.

—Yeah, I said.

She opened her eyes again.

—What do we do?

—I don't know.

—Where do we go? she asked.

—I don't know.

—My wrist hurts, she said. It was swollen, its skin bulging around the blue band.

—I know, baby.

She let out a small cry. She closed her eyes. A line of tears came down.

—Can we call Mom? she asked.

—No, baby, I said.

—But the phone. In my backpack, she said. She let out another small cry.

—I know.

—Why can't we call her?

—The phone won't work up here.

—They don't allow it to work up here?

—That's right.

—It's just us now? she asked.

—It's just us now.

Her eyes opened again. Her cries softened and then ceased.

—Where's the water? she said.

—There's some right here. I grabbed a bottle of sweetwater from the backpack and started to turn the top for her.

—No, I mean the sweetwater that was supposed to be here, she said. Why does it just smell like home?

Shelly looked over to the oilfields, to the east, that spread to the horizon just like the oilfields outside of Conrad and around Cut Bank. Her head turned to the west and to the darkness that still stuck there between the flares of orange and red. A line of cars with flashing lights was traveling through this darkness, heading east, traveling from the black into the predawn colors that have no name. The line of cars looked like the line of enforcers we'd seen the day before.

—Who are they? Shelly asked.

—I don't know, I said.

—Will they help us?

I watched them traveling east, their lights flashing red, white, red.

—Will they help us? she asked again.

—I don't know, baby.

—It's just us now? she said.

—Yeah, just us.

The line of cars turned south, turned toward us. Their flashing lights were dimming, the light from the east was building. There were trucks and in the trucks I could see men with masks, men with guns. The top half of the sun was up now, rolling sunlight over the plains, over the lights and the men that approached us.

—Is that okay? I said. Just us?

—Just us, she said.

—Yeah.

—Yeah, she said, and she touched her blue band and tried to spin it but it was too tight, her wrist too swollen, and she didn't say anything, she didn't mention the pain, didn't move to wipe that last tear falling over her cheek.

—It's good to have two, Shelly said.

—Two is good, I said.

—Twice as good.

—Sometimes even more, I said, hoping she still believed this.

We turned and watched the line of cars approaching us, their flashing lights glinting through the stars in the dusty windshield.

IN THE FLYOVER FICTION SERIES

Tin God
Terese Svoboda

Another Burning Kingdom
Robert Vivian

Lamb Bright Saviors
Robert Vivian

The Mover of Bones
Robert Vivian

Water and Abandon
Robert Vivian

The Sacred White Turkey
Frances Washburn

Skin
Kellie Wells

The Leave-Takers: A Novel
Steven Wingate

Of Fathers and Fire: A Novel
Steven Wingate

To order or obtain more information on these or other University
of Nebraska Press titles, visit nebraskapress.unl.edu.

CPSIA information can be obtained
at www.ICGtesting.com
Printed in the USA
LVHW112254240821
696043LV00005B/368